Edgar Wallace was born illegitimately in 1875 in Greenwich and adopted by George Freeman, a porter at Billingsgate fish market. At eleven, Wallace sold newspapers at Ludgate Circus and on leaving school took a job with a printer. He enlisted in the Royal West Kent Regiment, later transferring to the Medical Staff Corps, and was sent to South Africa. In 1898 he published a collection of poems called *The Mission that Failed*, left the army and became a correspondent for Reuters.

Wallace became the South African war correspondent for *The Daily Mail*. His articles were later published as *Unofficial Dispatches* and his outspokenness infuriated Kitchener, who banned him as a war correspondent until the First World War. He edited the *Rand Daily Mail*, but gambled disastrously on the South African Stock Market, returning to England to report on crimes and hanging trials. He became editor of *The Evening News*, then in 1905 founded the Tallis Press, publishing *Smithy*, a collection of soldier stories, and *Four Just Men*. At various times he worked on *The Standard*, *The Star*, *The Week-End Racing Supplement* and *The Story Journal*.

In 1917 he became a Special Constable at Lincoln's Inn and also a special interrogator for the War Office. His first marriage to Ivy Caldecott, daughter of a missionary, had ended in divorce and he married his much younger secretary, Violet King.

The Daily Mail sent Wallace to investigate atrocities in the Belgian Congo, a trip that provided material for his *Sanders of the River* books. In 1923 he became Chairman of the Press Club and in 1931 stood as a Liberal candidate at Blackpool. On being offered a scriptwriting contract at RKO, Wallace went to Hollywood. He died in 1932, on his way to work on the screenplay for *King Kong*.

The Lone House
Mystery

HOUSE OF
STRATUS

This edition published in 2001 by House of Stratus, an imprint of
House of Stratus Ltd, Thirsk Industrial Park, York Road, Thirsk,
North Yorkshire, YO7 3BX, UK.

www.houseofstratus.com

Typeset by House of Stratus, printed and bound by Short Run Press Limited.

A catalogue record for this book is available from the British Library
and the Library of Congress.

ISBN 1-84232-694-5

We would like to thank the Edgar Wallace Society for all the support they have given
House of Stratus. Enquiries on how to join the Edgar Wallace Society should be addressed to:
The Edgar Wallace Society, c/o Penny Wyrd, 84 Ridgefield Road, Oxford, OX4 3DA.
Email: info@edgarwallace.org Web: http://www.edgarwallace.org/

CONTENTS

THE LONE HOUSE MYSTERY

1

I am taking no credit out of what the newspapers called the Lone House Mystery. I've been long enough in the police force to know that the man who blows his own trumpet never gets into a good orchestra. So that, if anybody tells you that Superintendent Minter of Scotland Yard is trying to glorify himself, give them a dirty look for me.

"Superintendent" is a mouthful, and anyway, it is not matey. Not that I encourage young constables to call me "Sooper" to my face. They never do. I want "sir" from them and every other rank, but I like to overhear 'em talking about the old Sooper, always providing they don't use a certain adjective.

Mr John C Field always called me Superintendent. I never knew until he pronounced the word that there were so many syllables in it.

No man likes to admit he was in error, but I'm owning up that I broke all my rules when I liked him at first sight. It's all very well to go mad about a girl the first time you meet her, but it's wrong to file a man on your first impressions. Because a man who makes a hit the first time you meet him is going out of his way to make you think well of him. And normal men don't do that. Commercial travellers do and actors do, but they're not normal.

John C Field was the type that anybody could admire. He was tall, broad-shouldered and good-looking, for all his fifty odd years and his grey hair. He had the manners of a gentleman, could tell a good story and was a perfect host. He never stopped handing out the cigars.

I met him in a curious way. He lived in a smallish house on the banks of the Linder. I don't suppose you know the Linder – it's a stream that pretends to be a river until it runs into the Thames between Reading and Henley, and then it is put into its proper place and called the "Bourne." There is a house on the other side of the stream called Hainthorpe, and it was owned by a Mr Max Voss. He built it and had an electric power line carried from Reading. It was over this line that I went down to make inquiries. I was in the special branch of Scotland Yard at the time and did a lot of work that the county police knew nothing about. It is not an offence to use electric power, but just about this time the Flack brothers and Johnny McGarth and two or three of the big forgery gangs were terribly busy with private printing presses, and when we heard of a householder using up a lot of juice we were a bit suspicious.

So I went down to Hainthorpe and saw Mr Voss. He was a stout, red-faced man with a little white moustache, who had lost the use of his legs through frostbite in Russia. And that is how his new house came to be filled with electric contraptions. He had electric chairs that ran him from one room to another, electric elevators, and even in his bathroom a sort of electric hoist that could lift him from his chair into his bath and out again.

"Now," he said, with a twinkle in his eye, "you'll want to see the printing presses where I make phoney money!"

He chuckled with laughter when he saw he'd hit the right nail on the head.

I went there for an hour and stayed three days.

"Stay tonight, anyway," he said. "My man Veddle will give you any sleeping kit you require."

Voss was an interesting man who had been an engineer in Russia. He wasn't altogether helpless, because he could hobble around on crutches, though it wasn't nice to see him doing it.

It was pretty late when I arrived, so I did not need any persuasion to stay to dinner, especially when I heard that young Garry Thurston was coming. I knew Garry – I'd met him half-a-dozen times at Marlborough Street and Bow Street and other police courts. He had more endorsements on his driving licence than any other rich young man I know. His hobbies were speeding through police traps and parking in unauthorised places. A bright boy – one of the new type of criminals that the motoring regulations have created.

He had a big house in the neighbourhood and had struck up a friendship with Mr Voss. I suppose I'm all wrong, but I like these harum-scarum young men that the public schools and universities turn out by the thousand.

He stopped dead at the sight of me in the smoking room.

"Moses!" he said. "What have I done?" When I told him that I was after mere forgers he seemed quite disappointed.

He was a nice boy, and if I ever have the misfortune to be married and have a son, he would be the kind that would annoy me less than any other. I don't know what novelists mean when they write about "clean-limbed men," unless they're talking about people who have regular baths, but I have an idea that he was the kind of fellow they have in mind.

We were half-way through dinner when I first heard the name of Mr Field. It arose over a question of poaching. Voss remarked that he wished Field's policemen would keep to their own side of the river, and that was the first time I knew that Field was under police protection, and asked why. It was then that young Thurston broke in.

"He'll need a regiment of soldiers to look after him if something happens which I think is happening," he said, and there was something in his tone which made me look at him. If ever I saw hate in a man's eyes I saw it in Garry Thurston's.

I noticed that Mr Voss changed the subject, and after the young man had gone home he told me why.

"Thurston is not normal about this man Field," he said, "and I needn't tell you it's about a girl – Field's secretary. She's a lovely creature, and so far as I can tell Field treats her with every respect and deference. But Garry's got it into his thick head that there's something sinister going on over at Lone House. I think it's the psychological result of poor Field living in a place called Lone House at all!"

That explained a lot to me. Young men in love are naturally murderous young animals. Whether it's normal or abnormal to want to murder the man who squeezes the hand of the young lady you've taken a fancy to, I don't know. I guess it's normal. Personally speaking, I've never been delirious except from natural causes.

"Field's policemen" rather puzzled me till Mr Voss explained. For some reason or other Field went in fear of his life, and paid a handsome sum per annum for individual police attention. There were usually two men on duty near the house all the time.

I couldn't have come to a better man than Max Voss to hear all the news of the neighbourhood. I think that red-faced old gentleman was the biggest gossip I have ever met. He knew the history of everybody for twenty miles round, could tell you all their private business, why engagements were broken off, what made Mrs So-and-So go to the Riviera in such a hurry last March, and why Lord What's-his-name was selling his pictures.

And he told me quite a lot about Field. He lived alone except for a few servants, and had no visitors, with the exception of a negro who came about once a month, a well-dressed young fellow, and a rather pretty half-caste woman who arrived at rare intervals.

"Very few people know about this. She comes up river in a launch, sometimes with the negro and sometimes without him. They usually come in the evening, stay an hour or two and disappear. Before they come, Field sends all his servants out."

I had to chuckle at this.

"Sounds to me like a mystery."

Voss smiled.

"It is nothing to the mystery of Lady Kingfether's trip to North Africa," he said, and began to tell me a long story.

It was a pretty interesting story. Every time I woke up something was happening.

I went to bed late and tired, and getting up at six o'clock in the morning, dressed and went out into the garden. Mr Voss had told me his man Veedle would look after me, but devil a sign of Veedle had I seen, either on the previous night or that morning, and I understood why when I came upon him suddenly on his way from the little cottage in the grounds where he lived. He tried to avoid me, but I've got pretty good eyesight for a man of sixty. No man who had ever seen Veddle could forget him. A heavy-looking man with a roundish face and eyes that never met you, I could have picked him out a mile away. When Voss had said "Veddle," I never dreamed he was the same Veddle who had passed through my hands three times. Naturally, when criminals take on respectable employment they become Smith.

He knew me, of course.

"Why, Mr Minter," he said in his oily way, "this is a surprise!"

"Didn't know I was here, eh?" I said.

He coughed.

"Well, to tell you the truth, I did," he said, "but I thought it would be better if I kept out of your way. Mr Voss knows," he went on quickly.

"About your previous convictions?"

He nodded.

"Does he know that two of them were for blackmail?" I asked.

He smiled lopsidedly at this.

"It's a long lane that has no turning, Mr Minter. I've given up all that sort of thing. Yes, Mr Voss knows. What a splendid gentleman! What a pity the Lord has so afflicted him!"

I didn't waste much time on the man. Blackmail is one of the crimes that makes me sick, and I'd sooner handle a bushel of snakes than deal with this kind of criminal. Naturally I did not mention the conversation to Voss, because the police never give away their clients. Voss brought up the subject himself at lunch.

"That man Veddle of mine is an old lag," he said. "I wondered if you'd recognise him. He's a good fellow, and I think I pay him enough to keep him straight."

I didn't tell him that you couldn't pay any criminal enough to keep him straight, because there isn't so much money in the world, because I did not want to discourage him.

I saw Veddle again that afternoon in peculiar circumstances. He was always a bit of a dandy, and had considerable success with women of all classes. No man can understand the fascination which a certain kind of man exercises over a certain kind of woman. It isn't a question of looks or age, it's a kind of hypnotism.

I was taking a long walk by myself along the river bank. The river separated Mr Voss' property from the Lone House estate. Lone House itself was a square, white building that stood on the crest of a rising lawn that sloped up from the river, which is almost a lake here, for the stream broadens into what is known locally as the Flash.

A small wood on Mr Voss' side of the river hides the house from view. I was coming out of Fay Copse, as it was called, when I saw Veddle waiting by the edge of the stream. A girl was rowing across the Flash. Her back was turned to the servant, and she did not see him till she had landed and tied up the boat. It was then that he approached her. I was naturally interested, and walked a little slower. If the girl did not see Veddle, Veddle did not see me, and I was within a dozen yards of the two when he went up to her, raising his hat.

I don't think I've ever seen anybody so lovely as this girl, Marjorie Venn, and I could quite understand why Garry Thurston had fallen for her. Except for police purposes, I can't describe women. I can write down the colour of their eyes and hair, their complexion and height, but I've never been able to say why they're beautiful. I just know they are or they're not; and she was.

She turned quickly and walked away from the man. He followed her, talking all the time, and presently I saw him grip her by the arm and swing her round. She saw me and said something, and Veddle turned and dropped his hand. She did not attempt to meet me, but walked off quickly, leaving the man looking a little foolish. But it's very difficult to embarrass a fellow who's done three stretches for felony. He met me with his sly smile.

"A nice little piece that," he said – "A friend of mine."

"So it appears," said I. "Never seen anybody look more friendly than she did."

He smiled crookedly.

"Women get that way if they like you," he said.

"Who was the last woman you blackmailed?" I asked; but, bless you, you couldn't make him feel uncomfortable. He just smiled and went on his way.

I watched him, wondering whether he was trying to overtake the girl. He hadn't gone a dozen paces when, round the corner of a clump of trees, came swinging a man who I guessed was Field himself. You can tell from a man's walk just what is in his mind, and I wondered if Veddle was gifted with second sight. If he had been he would have run, but he kept right on.

I saw Field stand squarely in his path. He asked a question, and in another second his fist shot out and Veddle went down. To my surprise he made a fight of it, came up again and took a left swing to the jaw that would have knocked out any ordinary man.

It wasn't any business of mine, but I am an officer of the law and I thought it was the right moment to interfere. By the time I reached Mr Field, Veddle was running for his life. I was a little taken aback when Field held out his hand.

"You're Superintendent Minter? I heard you were staying in the neighbourhood," he said. "I hope you're not going to prosecute me for trespass – this is a short cut to Hainthorpe Station and I often use it. I don't know whether Mr Voss objects."

Before I could tell him I didn't know what was in Mr Voss' mind about trespassing he went on:

"Did you see that little fracas? I'm afraid I lost my temper with that fellow, but this is not the first time he has annoyed the young lady."

He asked me to come over to his house for a drink and, going back to where the skiff was moored, he rowed me across. We landed at a little stage and walked together up the lawn to the open French windows of his study. I noticed then that in front of these the grass was worn and that there was a patch of bare earth – it's funny how a police officer can register these things automatically.

The little study was beautifully furnished, and evidently Mr Field was a man who had done a lot of travelling, for all the walls were covered with curios: African spears and assegais, and on the shelves was a collection of native pottery. He saw me looking round and, walking to the wall, picked down a broad-bladed sword.

"This will interest you if you know anything about Africa," he said. "It is the Sword of Tuna. It belonged to the Chief of Ituri – a man who gave me a lot of trouble and who predicted that it would never be sheathed till it was sheathed in my unworthy person."

He smiled.

"I took it from his dead body after a fight in the forest, so his prediction is not likely to be fulfilled."

The blade was extraordinarily bright, and I told him that it must take a lot of work to keep it polished, but to my surprise he said that it was made from an alloy which always kept the blade shining – a native variety of stainless steel.

He replaced the sword, and for about a quarter of an hour we talked about Africa, where, he told me, he had made his money, and of the country, and only towards the end of our conversation did he mention the fact that he had a couple of detectives watching the house.

"I've made many enemies in my life," he said, but did not explain any further how he had made them.

He rowed me back to the other side of the Flash and asked me to dinner. I was going the following night. He was the kind of man I liked: he smoked good cigars, and not only smoked them but gave them to the right kind of people.

On my way back to Hainthorpe I met Mr Voss, or, rather, he nearly met me. The paths of his estate were as level as a billiard table and as broad as an ordinary drive, and they had need to be, for he drove his little electric chair at thirty miles an hour. It was bigger than a bath chair and packed with batteries, and if I had not jumped into the bushes I should have known just how heavy it was.

I did not think it was necessary to hide anything about Veddle, and I told him what I had seen. He was blue with rage.

"What a beast!" he said. "I have given that man his chance and I would have forgiven a little light larceny, but this is an offence beyond forgiveness."

Every afternoon he was in the habit of driving to the top of Jollyboy Hill, which gave him a wonderful view of the surrounding country, and, as he offered to put his chair into low gear, I walked up by his side, though it was a bit of a climb. From the top of the hill you saw the river stretching for miles, and Lone House looked a pretty insignificant place to be the homestead of a thousand acres.

In the opposite direction I could see Dobey Manor, an old Elizabethan house where Garry Thurston's ancestors had lived for hundreds of years.

"A nice boy, Garry," said Mr Voss thoughtfully. "Don't tell him about Veddle – I don't want a murder on my hands."

I dined with him that night, though I ought to have gone back to London, and he arranged that his car should pick me up at Lone House after my dinner and take me down.

"You are very much favoured," he said. "From what I hear, Field does not invite many people to his house. He is rather a recluse, and all the time I have been here he has not been to see me or asked me to pay him a visit."

I saw Veddle that evening. He had the most beautiful black eye I had ever seen on a man, but, as he did not speak about the little scrap, I thought I'd be tactful and say nothing.

I was just a little bit uneasy because Veddle was marked on the police books as a dangerous man. He had twice fought off detectives who had been sent to arrest him and had once pulled a gun on them. I happen to know this because I was one of the detectives.

In the morning I was strolling in the garden when I saw him coming from his little cottage, and thought it wise to offer a few words of advice.

"You got what you asked for," I said, "and if you are a wise man you'll forget what happened yesterday afternoon."

He looked at me a bit queerly. I'll swear it was one of the few times he ever looked any man in the eyes.

"He will get what is coming to him," he said, and turned immediately away.

That afternoon I sat on the terrace at Hainthorpe. It was a warm, drowsy day after a heavy shower of rain, and I was half asleep when I saw Mr Voss move along the path in front of the terrace in his electric chair. He was going very fast. I watched him till he disappeared in the little copse near the river's edge and saw the chair emerge on the other side and come up the winding path towards Jollyboy Hill.

Mr Voss always wore a white bowler hat and grey suit, and it was easy to pick these up even at a distance of a mile and a half, for, as I say, my eyesight was very good.

He was there longer than usual this day – he told me he never stayed more than ten minutes because he caught cold so easily. While he was there my eyes wandered to the copse, and I saw a little curl of smoke rising and wondered whether somebody had lit a fire. It was pretty hot – the sort of day when wood fires break out very easily. The smoke drifted away and presently I saw Mr Voss' chair coming down the hill and pass through the wood. A few minutes later he was waving his hand to me as he turned the chair on to the gentle incline which led to the front of the house. He guided the machine up to where I sat – the terrace was broad and stone-flagged.

"Did you see some smoke come over that wood? I thought the undergrowth was on fire."

I told him I had seen it. He shook his head. "There was nothing there, but I was a little alarmed. Last year I lost a good plantation through gipsies lighting a fire and forgetting to put it out before they left."

We talked for a little while and he told me he had made arrangements for his Rolls to pick me up at Lone House at ten.

"I hope you won't tell Garry about Veddle," he said. "I am getting rid of him – Veddle, I mean. I heard so many stories about this fellow in the village, and I can't afford to have that kind of man round me."

He questioned me about Veddle's past, but naturally I was cautious, for, no matter how bad a man is, the police never give him away. He knew, however, that Veddle had been charged with blackmail, and I thought it necessary that I should tell him also that this ex-convict was marked dangerous at headquarters.

He asked me to come into the house with him as Veddle had gone out for the afternoon, and I helped him into the lift and into the little runabout that he kept on the first floor. I was thoroughly awake by the time I got back to the terrace and sat down to read through a case which was fully reported in that morning's newspaper and in which I had an interest. I had hardly opened the paper before one of the maids came out and said I was wanted on the telephone. I didn't know the man who called me, but he said he was one of the detectives engaged to look after Mr Field. I didn't recognise the voice.

"Is that Superintendent Minter?... Will you come over to Lone House? Mr Field has been murdered..."

I was so surprised that I could not speak for a moment.

"Murdered!" I said. "Murdered?"

Then, hanging up the receiver, I dashed out of the house and ran along the path through the wood to the place immediately opposite Lone House. The detective was waiting in a boat. He was so agitated and upset that I could not make head or tail of what he was saying. He ran across the lawn and I followed him.

The French windows were wide open, and even before I entered the room I saw, on the damp, brown earth before the door, a distinct imprint of a naked foot. The man had not seen it, and I pushed him aside just as he was going to step on it.

I was first in the room and there I saw Field. He was lying in the centre of the floor, very still, and from his back protruded the hilt of the Sword of Tuna.

2

I didn't have to be a doctor to know that Field was dead. There was very little blood on the floor, considering the size of the sword blade, and the only disorder I could detect at the moment was a smashed coffee cup in the fireplace and a little table which had held the coffee service overturned on the floor. The second cup was not broken; the coffee pot had spilt on the carpet – when Field fell he might have overturned the table, as I remarked to the detective, whose name was Wills.

Now in a case like this a detective's work is usually hampered by a lot of squalling servants who run all over the house and destroy every clue that is likely to be useful to a police officer; and the first thing that struck me was the complete silence of the house and the absence of all servants. I asked Wills about this.

"The servants are out; they've been out since lunch time," he said. "Mr Field sent them up to town to a charity matinee that he'd bought tickets for."

He went out into the hall and I heard him call Miss Venn by name. When he came back: "She must have gone out too," he said, "though I could have sworn I saw her an hour ago on the lawn."

I sent him to telephone to his chief. I'm the sort of man who never asks for trouble, and there's no better way of getting trouble than interfering with the county constabulary. I don't say they are jealous of us at Scotland Yard, but they can do things so much better. They've often told me this.

While he was 'phoning, I had a look at Field. On his cheek was a wound about two inches long, little more than a scratch, but this must have happened before his death, because in his pocket I found a handkerchief covered with blood. There was nothing I could see likely to cause this wound except a small paperknife which lay on a table against the wall. I examined the blade: it was perfectly clean, but I put it aside for microscopic examination in case one of these clever Surrey detectives thought it was necessary. I believe in giving the county police all the help you can, and anyway it was certain they'd call in somebody from the Yard after they'd given the murderer time enough to get out of the country.

Leading from the study were two doors, one into the passage and the other into a room at the back of the house. On the other side of the passage was a sort of drawing-room and the dining-room. I say "sort of drawing-room" because it was almost too comfortable to be a real drawing-room.

I tried the door of the back room: it was locked. Obviously there was another door into the same room from the passage, but I found this was locked too.

When Wills came back from 'phoning – he'd already had the intelligence to 'phone a doctor – he told me the story of the discovery. He was on duty single-handed that afternoon; the second detective attached to the establishment had gone to town in Mr Field's car to the charity matinée. Wills said that be had been told to hang around but keep well away from the house, and not to take any notice of anything he saw or heard. It was not an unusual instruction apparently.

"Sometimes," said Wills, "he used to have a coloured woman and a negro lad come down to see him. We always had the same instructions. As a matter of fact, I was watching the river, expecting them to turn up. They usually arrived on a motor-boat from down-stream, and moored off the lawn."

"You didn't see them today?" I asked.

He shook his head.

"No; only the instructions I had today were exactly the same as I had when they were expected, and usually all the servants were sent out – and Miss Venn."

I made a quick search of the house. I admit that curiosity is my vice, and I wanted to know as much about this case as was possible before the Surrey police came in with their hobnailed boots, laying their big hands over all the finger-prints. At least, that's what I felt at the time.

I was searching Field's bedroom when Wills called me downstairs. "It's the deputy chief constable," he said.

I didn't tell him what I thought of the deputy chief constable, because I am strong for discipline, and it's not my job to put young officers against their superiors. Not that I'd ever met the deputy chief constable, but I'd met others.

"Is that you, Minter? Deputy chief constable speaking."

"Yes, sir," I said, expecting some fool instructions.

"We've had particulars of this murder 'phoned to us by Wills, and I've been through to Scotland Yard. Will you take complete charge of the case? I have your own chief constable's permission."

Naturally, I was very pleased, and told him so. He promised to come over later in the afternoon and see me. I must say this about the Surrey constabulary, that there isn't a brighter or smarter lot in the whole of England. It's one of the best administered constabularies, and the men are as keen a lot of crime-hounds as you could wish to meet. Don't let anybody say anything against the Surrey constabulary – I'm all for them.

My first search was of the desk in the study. I found a bundle of letters, a steel box, locked, and to which I could find no key, a loaded revolver, and, in an envelope, a lot of maps and plans of the Kwange Diamond Syndicate. I knew, as a matter of fact, that Field was heavily interested in diamonds, and that he had very valuable properties in Africa.

In another drawer I found his passbook and his bank deposit book and with these a small ledger which showed his investments. As near as I could gather, he was a half-a-million man. I was looking at this when Wills came in to tell me that Mr Voss was on the other bank and wanted to know if I could see him. I went down to the boat and rowed across. He was in his chair, and he held something in his hand which looked like a big gun cartridge.

"I've heard about the murder," he said. "I'm wondering whether this has got anything to do with it."

I took the cartridge from him; it smelt of sulphur. And then, from under the rug which covered his knees, he took an awkward looking pistol.

"I found them together in the copse," he said, "or at least, my servants found them under my directions. Do you remember the smoke, Minter – the smoke we saw coming from the trees?"

I'd forgotten all about that for the moment, but now I understood.

"This is a little smoke bomb. They used them in the war for signals," said Voss.

His thin face was almost blue with excitement.

"The moment I heard of what had happened at Lone House, I remembered the smoke – it was a signal! I got my chair out and came straight away down with a couple of grooms, and we searched the copse thoroughly. We found these two things behind a bush – and something else."

He dived again under the rug and produced a second cartridge, which, I could see, had not been discharged.

"Somebody was waiting there to give a signal. There must have been two people in it at least," he said. And then: "He is dead, I suppose?"

I nodded. He shook his head and frowned.

"It's queer. I always thought he would come to an end like that. I don't know why. But there was a mystery about the man."

"Where is Veddle?" I asked, and he stared at me.

"Veddle? At the house, I suppose."

He turned and shouted to the two grooms who were some distance away. They had not seen Veddle. He sent one of them in search of the man.

Veddle had been in my mind ever since I had seen the body of Field with the Sword of Tuna sticking through his back. I hadn't forgotten his threat nor his police record, and if there was one man in the world who had to account for every minute of his time that man was Mr Veddle.

"I hadn't thought of him," said Voss slowly.

He knitted his white eyebrows again and laughed.

"It couldn't have been Veddle: I saw him – now, when did I see him?" He thought for a little time. "Now I come to think of it, I haven't seen him all the morning, but he's sure to be able to account for himself. He spends most of his time in the servants' hall trying to get off with my housemaid."

A few yards beyond the copse was a small pleasure-house which had a view of the river, and this was equipped with a telephone, which the groom must have used, for he came back while I was talking and reported that Veddle was not in the house and had not been seen. Mr Voss brought his electric chair round, and I walked by its side back to the copse.

Locally it was called Tadpole Copse, and for a good reason, for it was that shape; large clumps that thinned off into a long tail, running parallel with the river and following its course downstream. It terminated on the edge of the property, where there was a narrow lane leading to the main road. It struck me at the time that it was quite possible for any man who had been hidden in the copse to have made a getaway without attracting attention even though the other bank of the river had been alive with policemen.

Voss went back to the house to make inquiries about his servant. He promised to telephone to me as soon as they were completed, and I returned to the boat and was ferried across to the house.

Two doctors were there when I arrived, and they said just the things you expect doctors to say…that Field had died instantly…that only a very powerful man could have killed him, and that it was a terrible business. They had brought an ambulance with them, and I sent the body away under Wills' charge and went on with my search of the desk.

I was really looking for keys. There were two locked rooms in the house, and at the moment I did not feel justified in breaking open any door until the servants returned.

I went round to the back of the house. The window of the locked room was set rather high and a blue blind was drawn down so that I could not see into it. Moreover, the windows were fastened on the inside. In all the circumstances I decided to wait till I found the key, or until the headquarters Surrey police, who were on their way, brought me a pick-lock.

Why had he sent his servants out that afternoon, and what could Marjorie Venn tell me when she came back? Somehow I banked upon the secretary more than upon the servants, because she would know a great deal more of his intimate life.

I went back to the desk and resumed my search amongst the papers. I was turning over the pages of an engineering report dealing with the Kwanga Mine when I heard a sound. Somebody was knocking, slowly and deliberately. I confess I am not a nervous man. Superintendents of police seldom are. If you're nervous you die before you reach the rank of sergeant. But this time I could feel my hair lift a little bit, for the knocking came from the door of the locked room.

3

There was no doubt about it: the sound of the knocking came from behind that locked door. I went over and tried the handle. I am a believer in miracles, and thought perhaps the knocker might have opened the door from the inside, but it was fast.

Then I heard a voice – the voice of a girl – cry "Help!" and the solution of that mystery came at once. I didn't wait for the keys to come; outside the kitchen door I had seen a big axe – in fact, I had thought that it might be useful in case of necessity. Going out, I brought in the axe and, calling the girl to stand aside, I had that door open in two minutes.

She was standing by a large, oriental-looking sofa, holding on to the head for support.

"You're Miss Marjorie Venn, aren't you?"

She couldn't answer, but nodded. Her face was like death; even her lips were almost white.

I set her down and got a glass of water for her. Naturally, as soon as she felt better she began to cry. That's the trouble with women: when they can be useful they become useless. I had to humour her, but it was about ten minutes before she could speak and answer my questions.

"How long have you been there?"

"Where is he?" she asked. "Has he gone?"

I guessed she was referring to Field. I thought at the moment it was not advisable to tell her that the late Mr Field was just then on his way to a mortuary.

"He's a beast!" she said. "He gave me something in the coffee. You're a detective, aren't you?"

I had to tell her I was a superintendent. I mean, I'm not a snob, but I like to have credit for my rank.

It took a long time to get the truth out of her. She had lunched alone with Mr Field, and he had become a little too attentive. Apparently it was not the first time that this had happened: it was the first time she had ever spoken about it. And it was only then she discovered that all the servants had been sent out.

As a matter of fact, she had nothing to tell me except what I could already guess. He had not behaved himself, and then he had changed his tactics, apologised, and she thought that the incident was over.

"I'm leaving tonight," she said. "I can't stand it any more. It's been terrible! But he pays me a very good salary and I couldn't afford to throw up the work. I never dreamt he would be so base. Even when the coffee tasted bitter I suspected nothing."

And then she shuddered.

"Do you live here, Miss Venn?"

I thought she was a resident secretary, and was surprised when she shook her head. She lodged with a widow woman in a cottage about half a mile away. She had lived at the house, but certain things had happened and she had left. It was not necessary for her to explain what the certain things were. I began to get a new view of Mr Field.

She had heard nothing, could not remember being carried into the room. I think someone must have interrupted him and that he must have come out and locked her in.

Wills admitted to me afterwards that he had come down to the house and that Field had come out in a rage and ordered him to go to his post.

I thought, in the circumstances, as she was calmer, I might tell her what had happened. She was horrified; could hardly believe me. And then she broke into a fit of shuddering which I diagnosed as hysteria. This time it took her some time to get calm again, and the first person she mentioned was Wills, the detective.

"Where was he – when the murder was committed?" she asked.

I was staggered at the question, but she repeated it. I told her that so far as I knew Wills was on the road keeping watch.

"He *was* here, then!" she said, so emphatically that I opened my eyes.

"Of course he was here."

She shook her head helplessly.

"I don't understand it."

"Now look here, young lady," said I – and although I am not a family man, I have got a fatherly manner which has been highly spoken of – "what is all this stuff about Wills?"

She was silent for a long time, and then, womanlike, went off at an angle.

"It's dreadful…I can't believe it's true."

"What about Wills?" I asked again.

She brought her mind back to the detective. "Mr Field was sending him away today. He only found out this morning that he is the brother of that dreadful man – the convict."

"Veddle?" I said quickly, and she nodded. "Did you know that it was Mr Field who prosecuted Veddle the last time he went to prison? Or perhaps you didn't know he'd been to prison?"

I knew that all right, as I explained to her.

"But how did he find out that Wills was Veddle's brother?"

Field had found out by accident. He was rowing down the river, as he sometimes did, and had seen the two men talking together on the bank. They were on such good terms that he got suspicious, and when he returned he called Wills into his study and asked him what he meant by associating with a man of Veddle's character, and Wills had blurted out the truth. He hadn't attempted to hide the fact that his brother was an ex-convict. In fact, it was not until that moment really that Field remembered the man.

"Mr Field told me," she went on, "that his attitude was very unsatisfactory, and that he was sending him away."

Just at that moment the deputy chief constable arrived by car and brought a crowd of bright young men, who had got all their detective science out of books. It was pitiful to see them looking for finger-prints and taking plaster casts of the naked foot, just like detectives in books, and measuring distances and setting up their cameras when there was nothing to photograph except me.

I told the chief all I knew of the case and got him to send the young lady back to her lodging in his car, and to get a doctor for her. One of his bright assistants suggested that we ought to hold her on suspicion, but there are some suggestions that I don't even answer, and that was one of them.

I went over with the deputy to see Mr Voss, who had sent a message to say that he had heard from Veddle. The man had telephoned him from Guildford. Half-way across the field he came flying down to meet us. I must say that that electric bath-chair of his exceeded all the speed limits, and the wonder to me was that he hadn't been killed years before.

There are some gentlemen who should never be admitted into police cases, because they get enthusiastic. I think they get their ideas of crime out of books written by this fellow whose name I see everywhere. He wanted to know if we'd got any finger-prints, and his red face got purple when I told him about the young lady locked in the room.

"Scandalous! Disgraceful! By gad, that fellow ought to be horsewhipped!"

"He's been killed," I said, "which is almost as bad."

Then I asked him about Veddle.

"How he got to Guildford in the time I haven't the slightest idea. He must have had a car waiting for him. It's the most astounding thing that ever happened."

"What did he say?" I asked him.

"Nothing very much. He said he would be away for two or three days, that he'd got a call from a sick brother. Before I could say anything about the murder he hung up."

I decided to search the cottage where Veddle lived. It was on the edge of a plantation, and consisted of two rooms, one of which was a sort of kitchen–dining-room, the other a bedroom. It was plainly but well furnished. Mr Voss, who couldn't get his machine through the door and shouted all his explanations through the windows, said he'd furnished it himself.

There was one cupboard, which contained an old suit and a new suit of clothes and a couple of pairs of boots. But what I particulaly noticed was that Veddle hadn't taken his pipe away. It was lying on the table and looked as if it had been put down in a hurry.

Another curious thing was a long mackintosh hanging behind the door. It was the longest mackintosh I have ever seen. On top of it was a black felt hat. I took down the mackintosh and, laying it on the bed, felt in the pockets – it is the sort of thing one does mechanically – and the first thing my fingers closed round was a small cylinder. I took it out. It was a smoke cartridge. I put that on the table and went on with the search.

One of the drawers of the bureau was locked. I took the liberty of opening it. It had a tin cash-box, which was unfastened, and in this I made a discovery. There must have been three hundred pounds in one-pound notes, a passport made out in the name of Wills – Sidney Wills, which was Veddle's real name – and a book of tickets which took him to Constantinople. There was a sleeper ticket also made out in the name of Wills, and the whole was enclosed in a Cook's folder, and, as I discovered from the stamp, had been purchased at Cook's west-end office the day before the murder.

There was a third thing in the drawer which I didn't take very much notice of at the time, but which turned out to be one of the big clues in the case. This was a scrap of paper on which was written:

"Bushes second stone's throw turn to Amberley Church third down."

I sent this to the deputy chief constable.

"Very mysterious," he said. "I know Amberley Church well; it's about eight miles from here. It's got a very famous steeple."

As I say, I didn't attach a great deal of importance to it. It was too mysterious for me. I put it in my pocket, and a few minutes afterwards I had forgotten it, when I heard that Wills, the detective, was missing.

4

The disappearance of Wills rattled me. And I'm not a man easily rattled. Now and again you meet a crook detective, but mostly in books. I knew just what they'd say at Scotland Yard – they'd blame me for it. If a chimney catches fire, or a gas main blows up, the chief constable says to the deputy: "Why isn't the Sooper more careful?"

Wills hadn't done anything dramatic: he'd just walked to the station, taken a ticket to London and had gone. I got on to the Yard by 'phone, but of course he hadn't turned up then, and I placed the chief constable in full possession of all the facts; and from the way he said: "How did that come to happen, Minter?" I knew that I was half-way to a kick. If I wasn't one of the most efficient officers in the service, and didn't catch every man I was sent after, I should be blamed for their crimes.

I got one bit of evidence. After I'd finished telephoning and come out of the house, I found an assistant gardener waiting to see me. He had seen Veddle walking towards his cottage about the time of the murder. He had particularly noticed him because he wore a long mackintosh that reached to his heels and a black hat; the mackintosh had the collar up and the tab drawn across as though it were raining. This was remarkable because it was a fairly warm day. The gardener thought he was a stranger who was trying to find his way to the house, and had gone across towards him, when he recognised Veddle.

"From which way was he coming?"

"From Tadpole Wood," said the man. "I told Mr Voss and he sent me on to tell you."

I liked Mr Voss: he was a nice man. But the one thing that rattles me is the amateur detective. I suppose the old gentleman found time hanging on his hands, and welcomed this murder as a farmer welcomes rain after a drought. He was what I would describe as a seething mass of excitement. His electric chair was dashing here and there; he was down in Sanctuary Wood with half a dozen gamekeepers and gardeners, finding clues that would have baffled the well-known Sherlock Holmes. He meant well, and that's the hardest thing you can say about any man.

He gave me one idea – more than one, if the truth be told. It was after I rowed across to Lone House and had come upon him and his searchers in the wood.

"Why do you trouble to row?" he said. "Why don't you get Garry Thurston to lend you his submarine?"

I thought he was joking, but he went on: "It's a motor-boat. I call it the submarine because of its queer build."

He told me that Garry had had the boat built for him to his own design. The river, though not an important one, is very deep, and leads, of course, to the Thames, where the Conservancy Board have a regulation against speeding. You're not allowed to use speeds boats on the Thames, because the wash from them damages the banks and has been known to wreck barges.

As Garry was keen on speed, and had taken a natural science degree at Cambridge, he had designed a boat which offered him a maximum of speed with a minimum of wash.

"It honestly does look a submarine. There's only about four feet of it above water, and the driver's seat is more like a conning tower than a cockpit."

"Where does he keep it?" I asked.

Apparently he had a boathouse about two hundred yards from the Flash. We afterwards measured and found that it was exactly two hundred and thirty yards in a straight line from Lone House.

Mr Voss was full of enthusiasm, and we went round the edge of the estate, touched a secondary road and in a very short time came to a big, green boathouse, but there was no boat there.

"He must be out in it," said Mr Voss, a little annoyed, "but when he comes in – there he is!"

He pointed to the river, and I'll swear to you that although my sight is as good as any man's I couldn't see it.

The boat was moving against a green background, and as it was painted green it was almost invisible. If I hadn't seen Garry Thurston's head and his big face I would never have seen it at all. The top was shaped like a sort of whaleback. The whole boat seemed to be awash and sinking.

He came up to us, moving very quickly, and Garry waved his hand to us, brought the boat alongside and stepped out.

"I've been down to the river," he said, "and nearly had an accident – Field's nigger friends were rowing up and they fouled my bow."

I had heard about these strange negroes who came to see Field occasionally, and I was very much interested.

"When was this?" I asked.

He told me. It must have been half an hour before the murder was committed.

"They were lying under the bank, and the boy evidently decided to row across into one of the backwaters, and chose the moment I was hitting up a tolerable speed for this little river. I only avoided them by accident. Why doesn't Field bring his native pals in a purdah car?"

I thought it was a bright moment to tell him that John Field had met his death that afternoon. He wasn't shocked, did not even seem surprised, and when he said "Poor devil!" I did not think he sounded terribly sincere. Then he asked quickly: "Where was Miss Venn?"

"She was in the house," I said, and I saw his face go pale.

"Good God!" he gasped. "In the house when the murder was committed – "

I stopped him.

"She knew nothing about it – that's all I'm prepared to tell you. At least, she said she knew nothing about it."

"Where is she now?" It was Voss who asked the question.

He was more shocked by the fact that the young lady had been locked in the room, although I had told him before, than he was by the murder.

"Where is she now?" asked Garry.

He looked absolutely ill with worry.

I told him that I had sent her to her lodgings, and I think he'd have started right away if I hadn't pointed out that it wasn't quite the thing to go worrying the girl unless she had given him some right.

"And anyway," I said, "she's a police witness, and I don't want her interfered with."

I told him what I'd come for, and told him at the same time that his boat was quite useless for the purpose: it was too long and too full of odd contraptions for me to bother my head about. But he had what I had thought was a row-boat, under a canvas cover, but which proved to be a small motor dinghy, and with this he ran me down to the Flash, showing me in the meantime how to work it.

I hadn't by any means got through Field's papers. In his pocket had been a bunch of keys. There was one odd-looking key for which I could find no lock. I discovered it that evening, when I was trying the walls of his study. Behind a picture, which swung out on hinges, I found the steel door of a safe. It was packed with papers, mostly of a business nature, and I was going through these carefully when Miss Marjorie Venn arrived. About tea-time I had sent her a note, telling her that when she was well enough I would like her assistance to sort out Field's papers. I didn't expect that she'd be well enough to come until the next day, but they telephoned, just before I began my search, to ask me if I would send the car for her.

She was quite calm; some of the colour had come back to her face; and I had a closer view of her than I had had that day on the bank, when Veddle had behaved like a blackguard. She was my ideal of what a woman should be: no hysterics, no swooning, just calm and sensible, which women so seldom are.

The servants had come back from the matinée, and I wanted to know exactly how I was to deal with them. She went out and saw them, and arranged that they were to stay on until further orders. A couple of the women, however, insisted on going home that night. She paid their wages out of money which she kept for that purpose.

There was no doubt about her being a help. She knew almost every document by sight, and saved me the trouble of reading through long legal agreements and contracts.

I sent for coffee when we were well into the work. It was while we were drinking this that she told me something about Field. He paid her a good salary, but she was in fear of him, and once or twice had been on the point of leaving him.

"I hate to say it of him, but he was absolutely unscrupulous," she said. "If he had not been a friend of my father's, and I was not obeying my father's wishes, I should never have stayed."

This was a new one to me, but apparently Field and Miss Venn's father had been great friends in South Africa. Lewis Venn had died there – died apparently within a year of Field finding his gold-mine.

"When Mr Field came back I was about fifteen and at school. He paid for my education and helped my mother in many ways, and after dear mother's death he sent me to Oxford. I had never met him until then. He persuaded me to give up my studies and come and act as his private secretary. I was under that deep obligation to him – " She paused. "I think he has cancelled that," she said quietly.

Her father and Field had been poor men, who had wandered about Africa looking for mythical gold-mines. One day they came to a native village and discovered, under a heap of earth, an immense store of raw gold, the accumulation of centuries, which the natives had won from a river, and which had been handed on from chief to chief.

"The Chief of Tuna," she said. "This sword – " She stopped and shuddered.

It was this that had put them on the track of the gold-mine.

"Mr Field often spoke about it."

She stopped rather abruptly.

"Now I think we ought to get on with our work," she said.

It was five minutes after this that we made a discovery. There was a false bottom to the safe, and in this was a long envelope, and, written on the outside: "The Last Will and Testament of John Carlos Field." The envelope was sealed down; I broke the seal and opened it.

It was written on a double sheet of foolscap evidently in Field's own hand, and after the usual flim-flam with which legal documents began, it said:

> "I leave all of which I die possessed to Marjorie Anna Venn, of Clive Cottage, in this parish – "

"To me?" Marjorie Venn looked as if she had seen a ghost. She evidently couldn't believe what I was reading.

"If you're Marjorie Anna Venn – "

She nodded.

"That is my full name."

She spoke like somebody who had been running and was out of breath.

"He asked me my full name one day, and I told him. But why – "

There was a big space under the place where he and the witnesses had signed, and here he had written a codicil, which was also witnessed.

> "I direct that the sum of five hundred pounds shall be paid to my wife, Lita Field, and the sum of a thousand pounds to my son, Joseph John Field."

We looked at one another.

"Then he was married!" she said.

At this minute one of my men came in to see me.

"There's a young man called. He says his name is Joseph John Field."

I pushed back my chair, as much astonished as the girl.

"Show him in," I said.

We didn't speak a word. And then the door opened, and there walked into the room a tall, young, good-looking negro.

"My name is Joseph John Field," he said.

5

Did I say I was not easily rattled? Well, I'm not. But I'd been rattled twice in one day.

I looked at the negro, I looked at Marjorie. The boy – he was about nineteen – stood there motionless; there was no expression on his face or in his brown eyes.

"Joseph John Field?" I said. "You're not the son of John Field, who was the owner of this house?"

He nodded.

"Yes, I am his son," he said quietly. "My mother was the daughter of the Chief of Tuna."

I could only look at him. I thought these kinds of cases only existed in the minds of people who wrote cinema stories. But there was this negro, making a claim that was so preposterous that I simply couldn't believe him.

"Then your grandfather was the Chief of Tuna – I suppose you know that the Sword of Tuna – "

He interrupted me.

"Yes, I know that."

"Who told you?" I asked sharply.

He hesitated.

"A detective. He telephoned to my mother tonight."

"Wills?" I asked.

Again he hesitated.

"Yes, Mr Wills. He has been a good friend of ours. He once saved my mother from – from being beaten by Mr Field."

"Is your mother black?" I asked. There was no time to consider his feelings, but apparently he was one of these sensible negroes who didn't mind being described as black.

He shook his head.

"She is negroid, but she is almost as pale as a European."

He had the cultured voice of an English gentleman. I found afterwards that he had been educated at a public school, and was at that time at a university.

"Mr Wills thought that I should come and see you, because, as mother and I were in the neighbourhood today, and we were known to have visited the house recently, suspicion might attach to us."

"It certainly does, young man," said I, and it was only then that I asked him if he'd sit down.

I could see Marjorie was listening, fascinated. The young man drew up a chair on the other side of the desk. He wore dark gloves and carried an ebony cane. His clothes were made by a good west-end tailor. He was in fact more like a real swell than any negro I've ever met. There was nothing ostentatious about his clothes, and, as I say, his voice was the voice of a gentleman.

He put his hand in his pocket, took out a leather case, opened it and handed me a folded paper. It was headed "March, 17th, being St Patrick's Day, 1907, at the Jesuit Mission, Kobulu." Written in faded ink were the words:

I have this day, and in accordance with the rites of Holy Church, performed the ceremony of marriage between John Carlos Field, English, and Lita, daughter of Kosulu, Chief of Tuna, and issue this certificate in proof thereof.

MICHAEL ALOYSIUS VALETTI, SJ

Underneath was written:

Confirmed. – MOROU, *District Commissioner.*

I handed the document mechanically to Miss Venn. She read it.

"This is your mother's marriage certificate," she said.

He nodded.

"You are Miss Marjorie Venn? I've never seen you before, but I know you very well. My mother knew your father. They came to our village more than twenty years ago, my father and yours."

I thought it was a pretty good moment to ask him about Field's life in Africa, but the boy would tell me nothing, except that Field behaved very badly to his mother and had brought a number of tribes with him to attack the village and had killed the Chief – his father-in-law.

I was a little knocked out to find a buck negro claiming to be the son of a white man, but if I'd had any sense, I'd have realised that this is one of the jokes that nature plays in marriages of mixed colour. It was understandable now why Field invariably sent his servants away when his wife and son called upon him.

My first inclination was to admire the man for having done the right thing by this coloured son of his, but then I realised that he could not very well do anything else. I didn't suppose his wife blackmailed him, but the possibility of the fact leaking out that this country gentleman was married to a negress would be quite sufficient to make him pay well to keep her quiet.

He could not even divorce her or allow her to divorce him without creating a scandal. I mentioned this fact to the boy, who agreed and said that Field had offered his mother a large sum of money to apply in the District Courts – I think they were Belgian – for a divorce, but his mother, having been mission-trained a Catholic, would not hear of divorce.

I wanted to get his reaction to the will, so I told him that he had been practically cut off, except for a thousand pounds. He wasn't a bit surprised, except that he had been left anything at all.

"Where did my father die?" the girl asked suddenly, but Joseph Field would say very little about what happened in Africa twenty-two years before. Possibly he did not know very much, though I am inclined to believe that he knew more than he was prepared to tell.

He did throw some sort of light on the cause of the quarrel between Field and the Chief of Tuna.

"My father had difficulty in locating the mine and came back and tried it again and again. He tried to persuade Kosulu – my grandfather – to let him have a share of the gold store which we kept in the village. Kosulu was Paramount Chief and the gold had been accumulating for centuries. It was to gain possession of this that he attacked the village – "

"Was my father in the attack?" asked the girl quickly.

Joseph Field shook his head.

"No, Miss Venn. The partnership had already been broken. Your father at the time was prospecting elsewhere. He did go back to the village after Kosulu was wounded and nursed him. John Field was bitterly disappointed because he had not been given the gold. He thought when he married my mother he would be able to take possession of the store. Mr Venn at that time was a very sick man. My mother tells me he was planning to go to the coast to make his way back to what you call civilisation" – I saw him smile; I guess he had his own idea of civilisation. "It was on his way to the coast your father died."

I cross-examined him as to the number of times he and his mother had visited Lone House, but I could get nothing that helped me very much. They had only come once without invitation and that was the time that Wills had to intervene to save the woman from John Field's hunting crop.

There was nothing for me to do but to take his name and address. He and his mother lived in a flat in Bayswater and I told him that I would call to see them on the first available opportunity.

"What do you make of that?" I asked the girl when he had gone.

She shook her head.

I thought she looked rather sad and wondered why; not that I spend much time in analysing the emotions of females.

"Isn't it tragic, that poor boy with all the instincts of a gentleman and the colour of a negro?"

I told her negroes did not really mind their colour, if they were good negroes, and only the third-rate coon gets his inferiority complex working because he happens to be of a different shade from the man who is being executed next week for cutting his wife's throat. There is just as much sense in a white man getting rattled because he doesn't match up with Paul Robeson.

We did not do much more searching, but spent the next hour discussing Joseph John Field, and the part he may have played. I told her I knew that they had been in the neighbourhood that day and where I had my information from. When I mentioned Garry Thurston she went very pink and started very quickly to talk about his boat.

"It's curious," she said. "Mr Field used to detest that motor-boat. I think it was because he hated being spied upon, as he called it, and he had an idea that Garry used to come down on to the Flash without being seen to – well, to see me."

"And did you see him very often?" I asked.

"He is a great friend of mine," she answered.

It's funny that you can never get a woman to give a straight answer to a straight question. However, it was not a subject that I wanted to pursue at the moment, so I let it drop.

The truth about John Field's relationship must come out at the inquest: I told Joseph that when I saw him off the premises, but he didn't seem much upset. It was clear to me that there was no love lost between him and his father. Generally when he referred to him he called him "John Field." I could see that the horsewhip incident was on his mind, and probably there were other incidents which nobody knew anything about.

It was easy to understand now why Wills was not popular with Field: he knew too much and probably presumed upon his knowledge. I guess that the woman must have told the detective that she was Field's wife.

An idea occurred to me suddenly.

"Do you mind if I ask you a delicate question, Miss Marjorie?" I said, and when she said no, I asked her if Field had proposed marriage to her.

"Three or four times," she said quietly, and I did not pursue the subject, because it might have been a very painful one for the young lady.

From what she told me it seemed that Field had lived almost the life of a hermit: he knew nobody in the neighbourhood and made no friends.

"Mr Voss asked him to dinner once, but he refused. He tried to buy Hainthorpe – "

Mr Voss' house?"

She nodded.

"He hated people living so close to him and he had an idea of building a house on top of Jollyboy Hill; in fact, he offered Mr Voss a very considerable sum of money through his agent for the hill alone, but the offer was not accepted."

There wasn't much more to be done that night. Mr Voss had asked me to stay with him and, after seeing the young lady home, I got one of our men who understands engines to take me across the Flash. Here I found the little two-seater which Mr Voss had put at my disposal: I don't understand motor-boats, but I can drive a car.

As I think I have explained, the house stands in a little stretch of meadow which is wholly encircled by trees. The path to the house is just wide enough to take a small car. The roads runs a little way through Tadpole Wood, through the thickest part of it. I was within a few yards of what I would call the exit, when I saw, by the reflection of my headlamps, somebody standing by the birch tree. Thinking it was one of the searchers, I slowed my car almost to a walk, and shouted: "Do you want a lift?"

I had hardly spoken the words before the figure straightened itself and fired twice at me.

6

The bullets stung past me so close to my face that I thought I had been hit. For a moment I stood paralysed with astonishment. It was the sight of the figure running that sort of brought me to life. I was out of the car in a second, but by this time he was out of sight. If I'd had the sense to bring my car round on a full lock, the lamps would have made it possible for me to see. As it was I was stumbling about in the dark with no chance of following my gentleman friend.

I think I ought to explain that Mr Voss had made dozens of "walks" in Tadpole Wood and there were paths running in all directions – a real laby— what's the word? Maze. I went back to the car and got my hand lamp, which I should have taken before. I ought to have known that any kind of search was a waste of time, but a man who's been fired at doesn't think as calmly as the chief constable sitting in his office (as I told him later). I hadn't any difficulty in finding where this bird had stood. I found the two shells of an automatic pistol lying on the grass. They were both hot when I found them. Naturally I kept them, because nowadays there is a new-fangled process by which you can identify from the cartridge the pistol that fired it, and I didn't think it was a satisfactory night's work. To go running through the wood was a waste of time – I realised that. The only hope was that the shots would have aroused one of Mr Voss' gamekeepers and that the man might be seen. Apparently it had aroused them, but in the wrong direction. Their cottages were on the other side of the house and I met them running over the ground on my way to Hainthorpe. By the time I told them what had happened, I remembered that I had two or three detectives at Lone House who would want to know all about the shooting, and I turned back to see them.

I was giving instructions about notifying the police stations around, with the idea of putting a barrage on the roads, when I heard two more shots fired in quick succession. They came from the direction of Hainthorpe. I got into the car again and flew up the road, not so fast as I might have done because I had police officers and gamekeepers piled into the machine or hanging on to the footboards.

The entrance of Hainthorpe is a great portico, and the first thing I saw in the lights of the motor lamps was a ladder lying across the drive. The house was in commotion. A servant, who looked scared sick, met me and asked me to come up to Mr Voss' room. He took me in the elevator. Mr Voss was sitting in bed. He was very red in the face, all his white hair was standing up and he was in his pyjamas.

"Look at that!" he roared and pointed to the curved bedhead.

It had been made of gilt wood, but now, for a space of about a foot, it was smashed to smithereens.

"They shot at me," he said.

(Did I say "he said"? He yelled it.)

"Look at that!"

Over the bed was a square hole in the wall that had shivered the plaster and sent it flying in all directions. The damage was so great that it didn't look like an automatic bullet that had done the work.

When he pointed to the French windows leading to the portico I understood why.

One window was smashed to smithereens, one was neatly punctured with a hole – both bullets must have started somersaulting the moment they touched the obstruction of the glass. I went out on to the top of the portico. It was surrounded by a low balustrade and had upon it a canvas awning – Mr Voss used to be pushed out here to enjoy the sunlight and sometimes, he told me, he had slept there.

One of the cartridge cases I discovered on the balustrade, the other on the drive below the next morning.

When I got Mr Voss quiet, he told me what happened. He had not apparently heard the first two shots that were fired at me, but he was awakened by the sound of a ladder being put against the portico. He sat up in bed and switched on the light.

"It was the most stupid thing I could have done, for the devil could see his target. The light was hardly on before – bang! I actually saw the glass smash…"

Though he was always regarded as a man of iron nerve, he was trembling from head to foot. One of the splinters from the wood had cut his right hand, which was wrapped up in a handkerchief. I wanted him to see a doctor about it, but he pooh-poohed the idea. I went downstairs whilst he dressed himself with the assistance of a servant, and after a while he came down the lift and wheeled himself into the library. He was much calmer and had enough theories to last him for the rest of the night.

I had all the servants in the house brought into the library one by one and questioned them. Nobody had seen the man who had done the shooting. The ladder was one belonging to the gardeners and was used in the orchard, but kept hanging near the house. I questioned everybody closely as to whether they had seen a pistol in the possession of Veddle. They were all very vague, except a gardener who had actually seen an automatic in Veddle's cottage. Mr Voss was very emphatic on the point.

"There was no doubt at all," he said, "he had a pistol: I saw him practising with it once and told him to throw it into the river." He told me then what he had never told me before: that in the course of the past year he had received two threatening letters written by anonymous correspondents.

"I didn't think it was worthwhile keeping them," he said. "They were written by some illiterate person, and I always suspected some gipsies I had turned off a corner of my land about this time last year."

"They were not in Veddle's handwriting?"

"No," he said slowly. "I don't think I have ever seen Veddle's handwriting now that you mention it."

I had the little scrap of paper in my pocket which I had taken from Veddle's cottage and I showed it to him. He examined the mysterious message it contained, reading out the words:

"Bushes second stone stop turn to Amberley Church third down."

I took the paper from him. I could have sworn that the third and fourth words were "stone's throw," but I saw I had made a mistake. Even with the change of the words it was as plain to me as it had been at first.

"I think that is Veddle's writing," he said. "What does it mean?"

"I haven't the slightest idea," I said. "The point is: is the writing anything like the anonymous letters you received?"

He shook his head.

"So far as I can remember, it isn't."

He pulled out another handful of letters from his pocket, trying to find some note which Veddle had written to him. He was one of those careless men who keep money, letters and odd memoranda in one pocket. As he went through them in search of the letter he threw half of them away.

"I get my pockets full of this stuff," he said. "It is what I call a bachelor's wastepaper basket."

I stooped and fished into the real wastepaper basket, and handed him something he had thrown away. They might have been old bills, they were so sprinkled with ink, but I've got an instinct for money.

"You may be a rich man," I said, "but there is no reason why you should chuck your money into the wastepaper basket."

They were bank notes, three for ten pounds and one for twenty pounds.

He chuckled at his carelessness.

"Perhaps that is why Veddle always took personal charge of my wastepaper basket. I wonder how much the rascal has made out of my carelessness."

It was nearly four o'clock when I went up to my room, after a long talk with the chief constable on the wire.

I am one of those old-fashioned police officers who never have got out of their notebook habit. Give me a bit of a pencil and a paper and I can collect all my thoughts on one page. Here were the facts:

1. A very rich man, occupying a lonely house by the river, is killed. The only immediate clue is the impression on the earth outside of a naked footprint.
2. In the house at the time of the murder and locked up in a room is his private secretary, a girl to whom he had been making love although he was a married man. It was impossible that she could have locked the door herself, for the key of the room was found in the dead man's pocket when he was searched.
3. One of the detectives engaged to look after Field disappears, and we discover that he is the brother of Veddle – Mr Voss' servant, a man who had a quarrel and a fight with Field and who threatened to get even with him.
4. Veddle and Wills disappear, but on the night following the murder, some person unknown appears in the grounds and fires at me and attempts to assassinate Mr Voss.
5. Mr Garry Thurston, who is in love with the secretary, possesses a boat which could approach the house unseen. He states, and this is confirmed, he was cruising along the little river at or near the time of the murder, and discovers a negress, who is Field's wife, and a young negro, who is Field's son, within striking distance of the house.

I wrote all this down, and the sun was shining through the windows by the time I had finished. I didn't feel like sleep. It's a queer thing – there is a point beyond which tiredness cannot go: you either drop into a heavy sleep where you sit, or you suddenly become as lively as a cricket. I had got to the cricket stage. I had a bath, shaved and, dressing myself, I went downstairs, unlocked the front door and stepped out. It was going to be a gorgeous day: the sun was up, the air was fresh and sweet. I decided to walk across the park towards Lone House. I knew the detectives would be there and some of them would be awake and could make me some coffee.

I stepped out very cheerfully, never dreaming that I was on the point of making a discovery which would change the whole complexion of the case.

As I think I told you, to reach the place where the river spreads out on a little lake one has to pass through Tadpole Wood. The birds were singing and it was the sort of morning somehow that you could not associate with police work, murders and midnight shootings.

I reached the spot where I had been fired at and, although I didn't expect to find anything, I had a sudden impulse to go off the path and make a search of the undergrowth. There was more than a possibility that I should find something which we had overlooked. I poked about with my stick in the undergrowth and in the grass and was turning to go when suddenly I saw two feet behind a bush; they were wide apart, the toes turned up. The man, whoever he was, must have been lying on his back.

I am not easily agitated, but there was something about these feet and their absolute stillness that sent a shiver down my spine. I walked quickly past the bush. Lying on his back was a man, his arms outstretched, his white face turned up to the sky. It was not necessary to see the blood on his throat to know that he was dead.

I stood looking at him, speechless. He was the one man I didn't expect to find murdered on that summer morning.

7

The dead man was Veddle. He had been shot at close quarters, and the doctor who saw him afterwards said he must have been killed instantaneously.

What struck me at the moment was that he had not been killed in the place he was found. His attitude, the fact that there was little or no blood on the ground, and the fact that I found afterwards traces of a heavy body being dragged to behind the bushes, all put the OK to my first impression.

I didn't do any searching at the moment, but, running through the wood, I came to the water's edge, intending to call assistance from Lone House. The first thing I saw was Garry Thurston's queer-looking boat. It was moored to the bank, the painter tied to a tree, and its stern had drifted out so that it lay bow on to the bank. One of our men was on the lawn, and I shouted to him to come over. He travelled across in the little motor dinghy.

"How long has that boat been there?" I asked.

"I don't know. I saw it a quarter of an hour ago when I came out on to the lawn, and wondered what it was doing there. It belongs to Mr Thurston, doesn't it?"

I wasn't worrying about the ownership of the boat at the moment, but took him up to the place where the body lay, and together we began our search.

He had heard nothing in the night, except that, just before daylight, he thought he heard the sound of a motor-car backfiring. It seemed a long way off, and nothing like the sound of the shots he had heard earlier in the evening.

Some rough attempt had been made to search Veddle's body, for the pockets of the jacket and the trousers pockets were turned inside out. It was in his hip pocket, on which he was lying, that we found the money – about two hundred pounds. The money was a bit of a shock to me, and upset all my previous calculations. It only shows how dangerous it is for an experienced police officer to make up his mind too soon.

"A hundred and eighty pounds," said the sergeant, counting it.

I put it in my pocket without a word.

We began to comb the wood, and in ten minutes we had found the place where the murder was committed. We should have known this by certain signs, but there was an already packed suitcase and an overcoat.

The place was about thirty yards from the drive which runs through Tadpole Copse, very near the spot where I had been shot at on the previous night.

There wasn't time to make more than a rough search of the suitcase, and that told us nothing.

I went down to the Flash and examined Garry Thurston's boat. The floor of the cockpit was covered with a rubber mat, of white and blue checks, and on these were the marks of muddy foot-prints. They weren't so much muddy as wet; it looked as if somebody had been wading in the water before they got into the boat.

Taking the motor dinghy, I went up to the boathouse. The gates facing the river were wide open; the little door on the land side was locked. I knew, because Garry Thurston had told me, that the gates opened automatically by pulling a lever on the inside of the boathouse, and they could only be opened from the inside. The boathouse itself was supported on piles, and I saw at once that it was possible for anybody who would take the risk to dive under its edge and climb up inside. I told the detective to take the suitcase across to Lone House, and, taking the police car, I drove up to Dobey Manor, where Mr Garry Thurston lived.

It was an old Elizabethan manor house, one of the show places of the county. I am not very well acquainted with the habits of the non-working classes, and I expected it would take me an hour to make anybody hear at that time of the morning. But the first person I saw when I got out of the car was Mr Thurston himself. He was up and dressed, and by the look of him I guessed he had not been to bed all night. He was unshaven, and his eyes had one of those tired, poker party looks.

"You're up early, Mr Thurston," I said, and he smiled.

"I haven't been to bed all night. In fact I've only just come in." And then, abruptly: "Have they found Veddle?"

That was the one question I didn't expect him to put to me, and I was a little taken aback. The one person I didn't think he would be interested in was Veddle.

"Yes, we've found him," I replied.

I looked at his face pretty straightly, but it was like a mask and told me nothing. He didn't speak for a moment, and then: "You found him, eh?" He spoke very slowly, as though he was thinking out every word carefully.

I expected him to ask me where Veddle had been found. I had an instinct that that was the question that was on his lips and which, for some reason, he dared not ask. I had come up to make inquiries about his motor-boat. It was merely a precautionary inquiry to clear up any possibility that he might have an arrangement with somebody in the neighbourhood to use the boat. But his attitude and his appearance changed my angle.

"Yes," I went on, not taking my eyes off him, "I found Veddle shot dead in Tadpole Copse."

He was a good-looking young fellow, but as I spoke his face went grey and old.

"You don't mean that!" It was almost in a whisper that he spoke. "Shot dead! Good God! How – how awful!"

It wasn't a moment to try to carry on a polite conversation – I put my question to him without trimmings.

"Where have you been all night, Mr Thurston?"

The colour returned to his face in large quantities. He made no attempt to deny the fact that he hadn't been in bed.

"I was just wandering around," he stammered. "I couldn't sleep – Veddle dead! How perfectly ghastly!"

Why was he so interested in Veddle, dead or alive? That puzzled me; but so many things had puzzled me in the past twenty-four hours.

He stopped further inquiries by saying: "Come inside and have some coffee," and, turning abruptly, he walked ahead of me through the garden, up a broad flight of steps on to the terrace before the house.

The first thing I saw on the terrace was something under a canvas cover that looked like a machine gun. He saw my eyes go in that direction, and I noticed him frown. He would have passed on, but I was curious.

"Oh, that!" he said, and was a little embarrassed. "That is a telescope. This house, as you see, is built on a rise, and on a clear day I can see objects forty miles away. If it wasn't for Jollyboy Hill one could see St Paul's well enough to tell the time by the clock."

It was a fairly clear morning. I pointed to a church spire about five miles away.

"What church is that?" I asked.

"That's Amberley," he said.

Amberley Church! I remembered the note that I had found in Veddle's room: "Bushes second stone stop turn to Amberley Church third down."

He seemed anxious to get me indoors, walked ahead of me, turning to see if I was following.

Generally speaking, I am not easily baffled, but the behaviour of this young man, his interest in Veddle, and the fact that he'd been out all night – the night that Veddle was murdered – upset quite a number of interesting theories that were beginning to sort themselves out in my mind.

It was when we were sitting in the big hall of his house, a room that looked like a small chapel, that I told him the reason I had come. He stared when I told him about the boat.

"I can't understand that," he said. "No, I haven't used the boat since – well, I haven't used it since you saw me on the river. Will you tell me where you found it?"

I described the position where the boat had been moored, and then, to my surprise, he asked: "Were any of Veddle's belongings on the bank or in the boat?"

When I told him about the suitcase I thought he turned a little pale. He certainly got up from the table quickly, leaving his coffee untouched, and paced up and down the room. I didn't know what to make of him. His agitation wasn't natural in a man who had nothing more than a casual interest in the death of Veddle.

I put the question again to him.

"What were you doing last night?"

"I went to town," he said.

There was a "you be damned" tone in his voice which was a little unexpected.

"Really, inspector, I don't see why my movements should be questioned."

"What time did you go to town?"

"At seven o'clock last night – it may have been eight. I didn't dine here."

I looked at his grey suit. He must have gone to town on pretty important business to have kept him up all night. I guessed then that he hadn't been back very long when I arrived at the house, but this guess was wrong, because I afterwards discovered he had returned at three o'clock.

There was no sense in alarming him. I put on my best jolly-good-fellow smile.

"Your coffee's getting cold, Mr Thurston," I said, helping myself to another cup. "If I've asked you any questions that I oughtn't to have asked I'm very sorry."

I drank up the coffee.

"I think I'll toddle back to Lone House and see what they've found in Veddle's suitcase. Have you seen Miss Venn lately – ?"

I had hardly asked the question when I heard a woman's voice behind me.

"Can I come in, please?"

I turned my head. Standing in the doorway was a woman. I guessed she was about forty. She was slim and tall, and dressed in a neat costume; and though she hadn't either the colour or the peculiar features of her race, I knew she was a negress and guessed she was John Field's wife.

8

The last person in the world I expected to see was the negress whom John Field had married in the wilds of Africa, and I was so taken by surprise that I hadn't a word to say. You can't imagine anything more – what is the word? incongruous, is it? – than the sight of that young woman in this big, vaulted manor hall. She just didn't belong to the country and didn't belong to the house.

The queer thing was that I had made up my mind during the night that I would see her that day.

I turned to Garry Thurston. I expected him to look embarrassed, but he wasn't.

"You don't know Mrs Field?" he said as calmly as you please. "I brought her down from town early this morning – her and her son."

It was one of those situations where a man can't exactly find the right word to break into a conversation. At least, I couldn't for a long time.

"Why did you bring her here?" I asked at last.

"Because I want to know something more about John Field – a great deal more than I know."

Now it is a fact that until that moment I had never considered this young man very seriously. I know his boat was seen in the vicinity of the house about the time the murder was committed, and one of my subordinate officers had suggested he should be questioned. But also I know quite a lot about criminals, and when you get an educated man committing a murder he doesn't as a rule fall into any of the errors that upset the applecart of the half-wits.

I looked from him to the woman. She had just realised who I was, and she was looking at me in a curious and understanding way. Mr Thurston beckoned her in and pulled out a chair for her.

"Now, Mr Thurston," I said, "perhaps you'll tell me what is it you want to know about Field? I may be able to put you right."

He shook his head.

"Nothing that I wanted to know about Field immediately concerns this murder," he said. "I was anxious to get particulars of his early life, and Mrs Field very kindly agreed to come down."

"Did you have to bring her down here, Mr Thurston? Couldn't you have questioned her in London?"

He shook his head.

"The questions I wanted to put had to be asked here," he said shortly, and I knew that nothing I could say would make him give me any further information, and I guessed from the look of the woman that she wasn't going to be helpful.

I put aside all the friend-of-the-family stuff, and began to ask him to account for his movements that night. And he had an alibi as fast as a rock. He'd been in town, and, what is more, his chauffeur had driven him and driven him back again. He couldn't have been anywhere near Tadpole Copse when the murder was committed. I don't think we were such good friends as we had been when I left, but he was the sort of young man who would know I was only doing my duty and would bear no malice.

I didn't go back straight to the house. It took my fancy to go up to the top of Jollyboy Hill. I've been too long in the police service to expect anything that looks or feels like inspiration, but I had an idea that once I got on top of that hill a lot of things would become clear that were at the moment a bit obscure.

Well, they didn't.

I walked down the other side of the hill, through Tadpole Copse, and stood there watching the local police while they were conducting a search which brought nothing to light except a towel. It was a curious thing to find in the bottom of a hollow tree. It hadn't been used very much, and looked to me as though it had not been long from the laundry, though it was crumpled and still damp. On the edge I found stitched one of those names that drapers sell to attach to laundry, and the name was "Veddle."

But the most important discovery of the morning was made by a detective officer of the Berkshire police, who took the dinghy down the river on the off-chance of finding some sort of clue. It's funny how amateurs expect to find clues strewed all over the face of the earth. But this fellow was lucky, for he found something that had a big bearing on the case. It was a sheet of paper floating on the water, and anybody who wasn't quite as enthusiastic as he was might have passed it by.

He sent the dinghy up to it and fished it out. It was a large date sheet, evidently torn from a calendar, and the date on it was the 4th of August in the current year. He would have thrown it back again but he saw on the back some writing in pencil, and, having read it, he brought the paper to me.

The first thing that struck me when I saw it was that I had seen a calendar that size before, but for the minute I couldn't place it. The writing on the back was in copying pencil and the water had made it very messy, but it was as easy to read as print. On the top was the number "23," and evidently this was the number of a page, for the writing started in the middle of a sentence.

"…have always kept my eyes open. And I kept my ears open too. I saw Field once in Tadpole Copse, but he saw me too and went back across the Flash. I went over two nights in succession and had a good look at the girl as she was leaving for her lodgings. I saw what I could do. If I married her my fortune was made, and I did my best to make up to her. After all, she was only a secretary and she didn't know…"

"She didn't know" were the last words on the paper. What didn't she know? To me it was fairly obvious. She didn't know that she was Field's heiress; but Veddle did.

What interested me about the sheet was that it was evidently part of a long story. Where were the other sheets? I sent the officer back in the dinghy to search the river as far as the Thames, and then I made my way up to the cottage where Veddle had lived.

Some busybody had been up to the house and wakened Mr Voss. I saw his mechanical chair whizzing down the path towards me, and from the fact that he still wore his pyjamas and a dressing-gown I guessed he'd only just got out of bed.

"Is it true about Veddle? When did it happen? Why didn't somebody wake me up?"

I couldn't answer all the questions he put to me, but I told him that I was going to search the cottage and asked him if he would lend me the key. He blew a whistle, and one of his gardeners came running forward and was sent back to the house to get the key, whilst we went on to the hut. I call it a hut although it was brick made and thatched.

We had to wait a little time until the gardener returned, and I told Mr Voss as much as I thought he ought to know. He was very thoughtful.

"He must have been in the grounds last night. Do you think it was he who fired at us?"

I couldn't answer that question till the door of the cottage was opened. When I walked in, however, there was the answer on the table – a Browning pistol, the barrel still foul from the shot that had been fired, and seven unused cartridges in the magazine.

The room was just as I had left it, except (I remembered now) that the big calendar I had seen on one of the walls was lying on the table. The sheets had been torn off as far as September 7th. The back of the sheets were blank and could be used for writing paper. I had no doubt that Veddle had used it for that purpose.

The pen and ink were still on the table. How had he obtained admission? I went to the door – Mr Voss could not come in because of the narrowness of the passage – and asked him if there was another key. He shook his head.

"He could easily have had one made, but I know of no other," he said.

I was returning to the room when he called me back.

"It has just occurred to me that he may have been there all the time."

"Whilst I was searching before, you mean?"

He nodded.

"Yes. There's a large cellar underneath the house. I think it was used for storing wine in my predecessor's days. It's queer I never thought of that before. You'll find a trapdoor in the bedroom."

I made a search of the bedroom, turned up the carpet, and sure enough there was the trap! A wooden ladder led to the bottom, and it only needed a casual examination to show that the cellar had been lived in and slept in, for there was a camp bed, half a dozen blankets and a small electric handlamp, the sort you can buy for five shillings at any store.

So that was where Veddle had hidden. The place was well ventilated, and he could have stayed there, without anybody being the wiser, for a week. I found a tin of biscuits, half-a-dozen bottles of mineral water, and the half of a Dutch cheese in a small cupboard behind the bed.

There was no other clue. I came up the steps, and, closing the trap, whistled for an officer to stay on duty in the cottage until he was relieved. Mr Voss and I went back to the house together. I had to telephone to the chief constable and arrange for a couple more of my men to come down.

Mr Voss had to take his chair by another route. He ran up a long incline to the terrace, but he was waiting for me by the time I got up the steps. And then he made a suggestion which staggered me. When I say it staggered me, I am probably giving you a wrong impression. Nothing staggers me, but it was certainly unexpected.

"Is it possible to keep the story of the Veddle murder out of the newspapers?" he asked.

"Why on earth, Mr Voss?"

He looked at me very thoughtfully.

"You'll probably think that I'm not quite right in my head, but I have a theory that if this news is suppressed today, the murderer will be in your hands tomorrow morning."

He would give me no reason. I hate people who are mysterious, because in nine cases out of ten they've nothing to be mysterious about. And then I told him about the piece of paper that was found on the river. I have been told by the chief constable that I am a talkative old man. Maybe I am; but I have found that the worst way to get through a case like this is keeping your mouth shut, and I thought this was the moment to talk.

He took the paper which I had in my pocket and examined it.

"Yes, that's Veddle's writing," he said at last; "obviously part of a long confession. I wonder what happened to the rest of it?"

That was the one thing I intended finding out.

9

I took the letter into his study and examined it carefully, and then, with Mr Voss' permission, I sent for his steward, or butler, or whatever he was called. I had seen a telephone in the cottage, and I had meant to ask before whether that 'phone was fixed up to the house exchange. When the steward told me it was not, a lot of light was thrown on the mystery of Veddle's death.

I got through to the local telephone supervisor and asked a few questions. Naturally he couldn't answer, because he'd only just come on duty; but an hour later, when I was having breakfast, I was called for. The supervisor had got all the data I wanted. A message had come through at about ten o'clock on the previous night from the cottage 'phone, obviously from Veddle, who had asked for a London number. They had talked for six minutes, and the operator had no idea to whom he was speaking. There was a record of the call, and I got straight through to the number and found it was a small hotel near Paddington Station. Nobody named Wills was staying there, but the night porter had left a record that a "Mr Staines" had been rung up at something after ten, and that it was a toll call. "Mr Staines" himself was not in the hotel at the moment I 'phoned. I took no risks, but got through to the Yard immediately and sent a couple of officers to pick up "Mr Staines" and see how much like Mr Wills he looked. When I came back I found Mr Voss had hatched out a brand-new theory, and it was so very much like my own that I wondered if I'd been talking aloud to myself.

"I'm sure this man Wills is in it," he said. "I shouldn't be surprised if he was the fellow who stole Garry Thurston's boat – my butler was telling me it was found moored on the Flash."

"In that case," said I, "Mr Wills has got the last dying speech and confession of his brother. But why he went away without Veddlc is a mystery to me."

Voss returned to the subject of publicity, and he was very earnest.

"You have to realise, Sooper," he said, "that I have a scientific mind. I may not be a good detective, but I have the faculty of deduction. Since I lost the use of my legs I've spent my time working out problems more intricate than this, and I am more satisfied than ever that if you keep the shooting of Veddle out of the newspapers you'll have your man tomorrow morning."

"Are you suggesting that Wills killed him?" I asked.

He shook his head.

"Of course not! Wills is obviously a confederate. He came up the river, probably by boat, last night, to get his brother away. You've been making inquiries at the exchange, haven't you? Without having stirred from this room or being told by any person who overheard your conversation, I can tell you you have been asking what were the messages that passed between the cottage and some unknown destination last night."

I grinned at this.

"Oh, no, I'm not guessing, I'm telling you," said Mr Voss, his face getting pinker and pinker, his white hair almost standing up on his head in his excitement. "And I'll bet you found that it was his brother he called – or, if you haven't, I can tell you it was! He asked his brother to come down and get him away. His brother arrived by boat."

"Why not by road?" said I.

"The roads are under observation, aren't they? What chance has a car of getting within a mile of this place? No, he came by river, probably by row-boat – he must have had a row-boat to have got out into the stream and stolen Garry Thurston's odd little launch. He brought that launch down to where you found it, and met his brother, who probably went back to the cottage for his suitcase or something of the sort. Did you find any suitcase, by the way? I see you did. He may have handed over the story of the crime to Wills, who rowed downstream ahead of the motor-boat and got away, quite confident that his brother would escape."

"I don't see the object of holding this story from the newspapers," I said.

"Don't you?"

Max Voss' voice was very quiet.

"I do! Two people have been killed, both by the same hand." He tapped on the tablecloth, emphasising every point. "The one person who knows the murderer is Wills. Publish the news that Veddle has been found killed and Wills will come into the open – and will go the same way as Field and his brother!"

That was a brand-new angle to me. It never occurred to me that Wills was hiding from anybody but Superintendent Minter. Personally, I don't like my theories upset by other people. Nothing annoys me more than to work out a case so that every little bit of the puzzle fits, and then for somebody to show me I've got one piece upside down. But Mr Voss was a man for whom I had a great respect, and the more I saw him the more I respected him. I don't believe in amateur detectives, the kind you read about in books, but if I had to work with one of those well-known sleuths I'd like him to be as near to Mr Voss as possible, because undoubtedly he had brains.

I thought Marjorie Venn was late when she turned up at Lone House that morning, but the truth was I had been up so early that ten o'clock seemed the middle of the day. I had taken a copy of the writing on the paper, and I showed it to her. She was puzzled, though she remembered several occasions when Veddle had tried to get acquainted with her. She had once paid a visit to a cinema house in Reading (it was on a Saturday afternoon and she had gone into Reading by the 'bus) and found Veddle sitting by her side.

I didn't tell her for some time about the man being dead. In fact, she got it from one of the servants in the house and came to me very distressed. I could see the business was getting on to her nerves, and I was wondering whether I couldn't get her away from the place to

London. Mr Field's lawyer was coming that day, and as she inherited Field's money she could afford to stay at the best hotel in town, and I knew that the lawyer would advance the cash. When I made the suggestion, however, she wouldn't hear of it.

It was a casual reference I made to Garry Thurston which explained why she didn't want to leave the neighbourhood. I saw a flush come to her face, and I guessed that she and Garry were better friends than either of them had admitted.

I think she may have surmised my suspicion, for she very quickly got away from the subject of this young man.

"I'm not at all nervous, and I'd rather stay in the country till this ghastly murder is settled," she said. "And I wouldn't dream of leaving until I have all Mr Field's affairs in order."

That afternoon I had a blow. Our chief constable is as kind a man as you'd meet in a day's march, but he is not what I would call a very sensitive man. Because, if he had been, he wouldn't have sent Superintendent Gurly to exercise, as he called it, a general supervision. Gurly is my senior. I've nothing to say against him; I daresay he's a good father and a moderately good husband. He's fat and I don't like fat men, but I've known fat men who I could get on with. I never could get on with Gurly, ever since we were constables together. He was the sort of man who knew everything, except how little he knew; and naturally, the first thing he did when he came on the spot was to take charge of everything, give orders to my men and generally make himself conspicuously useless.

I have been on many cases with Superintendent Gurly, but never found a way of getting over him. If you threw up the case and went back to the Yard, it meant you had to go back to undo all his well-meaning work a few days later. If you complained to the chief constable, the chief would say: "Well, you know what he is – just humour him."

He fussed about the house till late in the afternoon, and then he came and said: "I think I'll take a dinghy and row down the river, Minter."

"Can you swim?" I asked, but even when he said "No," I knew it was no good hoping, because fat men float.

I arranged to sleep at Lone House that night, and by the time dinner was over Gurly came back as full of ideas as a bad egg is full of bouquet. Marjorie Venn had gone back to her lodgings, so that I could use all the bad language I wanted to use without hurting anybody's feelings. Anyway, you couldn't hurt Gurly with a hatchet. If ever I wanted to murder the man, it was when he said: "I've got all the threads in my hand now, Minter – in fact, I think I could execute a warrant in the morning."

"Fine," I said. "You naturally *would* know everything in half-an-hour. Who killed John Field?"

He looked at me and waggled his head, and I know that when Gurly waggles his head he's going to be so silly that you have to laugh or be sick.

"A girl," he said.

I just gaped at him.

"Who? Miss Venn?"

He nodded.

"Is anything more obvious?" he asked. "I wonder it hasn't occurred to you before, Minter."

He leaned over the table, and he's so fat that the table creaked. I was creaking a bit myself.

"She was in the house when the murder was committed – you don't deny that. She was locked in the room, I grant you, but what was to prevent her from locking the door and throwing the key out of the window?"

"The only thing that was likely to prevent her was that the key was in the dead man's pocket," I said, but that didn't choke him off.

"There may have been two keys, or three," he said. "Who benefited by his death? She did! It's pretty well established that she disliked him, Minter. She was having an affair with somebody in the neighbourhood – I haven't found out who it was – "

"You should have taken another five minutes," I said; but, bless your soul, that kind of kick never reached him.

"He was killed by the Sword of Tuna – " he began again, when I stopped him.

"The man who killed John Field left his naked footprint outside the door. It wasn't a woman, it was a man. Get that silly idea out of your head, Gurly."

"There are one or two questions I'm going to ask her," he said, and took out of his pocket a big notebook, which he must have spent hours filling up. "Will you bring her in?"

"She's gone," I said very coldly.

"Then she's got to be brought back."

10

Now when Gurly is in that kind of mood there's no coping with him. He was perfectly within his rights in wanting to question Marjorie Venn, and I had no authority to stop him. For one thing, it would have looked pretty bad in his report if I had put any obstacle in his way; so, after trying to persuade him to leave the matter over till the morning, I agreed to go down with him to the cottage where she lived and see her.

"She may be gone in the morning," said Gurly.

It was a waste of time answering.

A police car took us to the little village where Marjorie Venn lived with a widow woman who kept a small shop. Marjorie had the two best rooms in the house, and had furnished them herself, she told me.

The shop was shut, but we knocked up the landlady and told her what we had come about. She looked at us in surprise.

"Miss Venn has gone to London – she went half an hour ago, and took all her things with her – she's not coming back."

I couldn't believe the news that Marjorie Venn had gone without saying a word to me, especially after all she had told me that afternoon. I had done my best to persuade her to go to London, but she had said she was staying until John Field's affairs were cleared up; and here, without the slightest warning, she had disappeared.

"What did I tell you?" said Gurly. "I knew it, my boy. You oughtn't to have let her out of your sight – "

I didn't take any notice of him.

"How did she leave? When did she make up her mind?" I asked the widow.

According to her story, a note had been delivered to her and she had gone out immediately, not even putting on her hat. She was gone a quarter of an hour, and when she came back she seemed agitated and went straight up to her room and began packing. The landlady knew this because she had gone up with a glass of milk which the girl usually took before she went to bed. She found her putting her things into a suitcase, and Marjorie told her she had been called to London on very urgent business, and that a car was coming for her. It arrived a few minutes later.

Exactly what kind of car it was the landlady could not say, because it had driven through the village and had pulled up by the side of the road, and all that she saw was its tail light. Marjorie had carried her own suitcase to the car, and paid the woman her lodging money, and that was all the landlady knew.

I went to the village inn, but could find nobody who had seen the car. Even the village policeman could give me no information. Although the place was not on the highway to anywhere, cars frequently passed through the street.

The news knocked me out, but old Gurly was chortling with joy.

"What did I tell you?" he shouted. "She's bolted! She knew I was here, of course – "

"That's enough to make any woman bolt," I snarled at him, "but not a girl like Miss Venn."

We took the car on to the first police control post, but they could tell us nothing. Any number of cars had passed, none of them so suspicious looking that the sergeant in charge felt called upon to pull it up.

"The car might have taken a circuitous route," suggested Gurly, and for once in a way his was an intelligent suggestion.

There were half-a-dozen by-ways, but unless the car was moving in a circle it must pass one of the "barrages."

Driving back to the house, Gurly let himself go – he was more Gurlyish than ever I remember him.

"It's the obvious things that always escape the ordinary police officer's attention," he said. "The moment I came into the house, my suspicions were on that girl. I worked it out a dozen ways, and I came to the conclusion that the only person who could have killed Field – "

"And shot Veddle?" I suggested.

"Why not?" said Gurly.

He was the sort of man who, when he gets into an argument and finds himself cornered, raises his voice to a shout. I kept him shouting all the way back to Lone House.

So far as I knew, the girl had no friends in London and the only thing to do was what Gurly did – circulate a description to the hotels and ask for notification of her arrival. Gurly would have sent out an "arrest and detain" order, but I stopped that. After all, he's a member of the police force, and I didn't want Scotland Yard to look foolish.

From all our searchings and examinations that day, one or two important facts had come to light. The first of these was that Veddle was the man who had shot at me and at Max Voss. He had used an automatic; the back fire from the cartridge had burnt and blackened his hand. He had made some attempt to get the stain off, but it was very visible; and to prove my theory I found, on a re-search of the cottage, a spare box of ammunition.

We went over together, Gurly and I, and at Mr Voss' invitation went up to the house to supper. Before we went in I told the superintendent of Mr Voss' request, and naturally he took the opposite view to me.

"I quite agree – there's too much publicity about police affairs, Minter. The reporters would only have come down and got a sensational story, and taken away all the credit that's coming to me."

Now, the curious thing about the Lone House murder was that we'd only had two local reporters on the job. As a rule, in cases like these the whole countryside is over-run with newspaper fellows; but you've got to remember that it wasn't called "The Lone House Mystery" in the first two or three days.

Only four people outside police circles knew how the murder had been committed – even the servants knew no more than that Mr

Field had been found dead, for they were all out at the time of the murder, and we tied them all up to secrecy by promising them that they wouldn't lose their jobs (Miss Venn did that for me) if they kept quiet.

So I didn't think the story had reached the press, though I found later that one of the local reporters had 'phoned a column to an evening newspaper.

There was another reason why I thought the press would miss the Veddle killing. Big police cases usually go in threes, and just then the Tinnings case was holding down a lot of space in the newspapers – it was a poison murder, and a fashionable actress was in it, and, as I happened to know, most of the star men of the London press were quartered in a little town to the north of London, where the suspect lived. But, as I say, I was wrong.

One of the first questions Mr Voss asked me when I went in, was whether there was anything about Veddle's murder in the evening newspapers. He had had them all sent down from London, and they contained no reference to the crime, but he was worried as to whether they were in the later editions. I wasn't in a position to tell him, because I never read newspapers except when they contain the account of a trial where I have been specially commended by the judge.

It was the next day that I found that the murder had been splashed on the front page of an evening newspaper.

Naturally, Gurly and Mr Voss became boy friends. Gurly has got a weakness for monied people. I had asked him not to discuss the case with Voss, because, as I told him, I didn't want him worried; but we hadn't been seated at the table for five minutes when Gurly started throwing off his theories and deductions.

"You know the girl, Mr Voss?"

Voss looked at him quickly.

"Miss Venn? Yes – why?"

Gurly smiled and spread out his fat hands.

"Who else could it be?"

I thought that Voss was going to have a fit.

"You don't mean to tell me that you suspect Marjorie Venn – "

I think he was going to say something rude, but he checked himself.

"Yes, I do," said Gurly; "and the fact that she's disappeared tonight – "

Voss pushed himself back from the table, staring at my thick-headed colleague.

"Disappeared? What do you mean – ?"

I thought it was time to step in. "She's gone away, Mr Voss – left at a few minutes' notice."

"When was this?"

He reached out his hands, gripped the edge of the table and pulled the wheel chair back to where it had been, and he seemed to have got the better of his annoyance.

Gurly told him, because Gurly is the sort of man who must speak or perish.

"Just tell me what happened to this young lady," Voss interrupted him. "I am very much interested in her; in fact, I had thought of asking you to introduce me. She may want work – "

"Work!" said Gurly. "My dear fellow, that's the whole point – she's his heiress."

"Field's?"

I never saw such a blank look of unbelief in a man's face.

"He left her all his money," Gurly went on, rushing down the road marked 'Angels only.' "That's my point! She had everything to gain by his death…"

He ambled on, but Voss wasn't listening to him. He was staring at me.

"You never told me this, Mr Minter," he said. "It is amazing news. Why did he leave her the money? Was there anything – wrong?"

Each question came like the snap of a whip, and as I didn't want Gurly to explain, I told him just as much as I thought an outsider ought to know. I saw the relief in his face before I had finished.

"Conscience, eh? The girl's father was his partner, you say? This rather complicates matters."

"Upsets your pet solution?" I asked him, and he nodded.

Then without warning he switched on to another subject.

"Have you seen Garry Thurston? He hasn't been up today. I think he ought to know about Miss Venn's disappearance – have you told him?"

He snapped his finger at the butler, who came back with a telephone; it had a long cord attached, and at the end a plug which he pushed into a socket in the wall.

I didn't say anything; I was anxious to know just what Mr Garry Thurston would say, and would have given anything to listen in and discover his reaction – that's the word, isn't it?

Voss jiggled the hook impatiently and presently he got through. He asked one or two questions, and I could tell he was talking to the servant.

"Garry's gone to bed." He covered the receiver with his hand. "Do you think I ought to get him up?"

Before I could reply he was speaking again. "Yes. Tell him I want him. It's very urgent."

He waited some time, and then: "Hullo! Is that you, Garry? It's Voss speaking."

He was silent for a while, evidently listening to what Thurston was saying at the other end.

"Yes," he said at last, and then again: "Yes."

Once he started to interrupt Thurston, but he did not ask the question which I knew was on his lips. I saw his face go paler, and his bushy eyebrows meet, but he said nothing which would tell me what the conversation was all about. Then, to my surprise, he said "All right," and hung up the receiver. He handed the instrument to the butler and met my eye.

"Well," said I, "you didn't seem to let him know very much about Miss Venn?"

He had no answer at once, but sat looking at me for quite a long time.

"No, I didn't ask him any questions: he told me all I wanted to know," he said. "Miss Venn went to London on Garry Thurston's advice. She went because he thought there was danger to her and – "

Bang!

The glass in the big oriel window smashed and splintered. Something hit the decanter in front of him and cut the neck off as though it had been sliced by a knife. For the second time in twenty-four hours somebody had shot at him.

11

How quickly can a man think? Not a second had passed between the shot being fired and the moment I jumped to my feet, but I had followed nearly twelve thousand miles, I had lived over the life of Field and had gone over every aspect of his killing – and I knew the murderer. I knew him as I stood by that table, half twisted round towards the smashed window. I knew just why that smoke signal had been used in Tadpole Copse, and why I had found the print of the man's foot on the soft earth outside Field's study.

A second? It could not have been a tenth of a second. I'll do Gurly justice: he was out of that room before I could say "knife," and I was not far behind him. We flew into the hall, over the terrace – there was nobody in sight. The grounds were as black as pitch; we could see nothing. Our only hope was that the couple of men we had left on duty patrolling the river bank near the copse would have heard the shot and might have seen the man who did the shooting, but although they hurried up to the house, they had met nobody.

It was nearly one o'clock before I left Voss. I intended putting my men inside the house, but Gurly wouldn't hear of it.

"I'll stay with Mr Voss," he said, "and if I am not as good as any two flat-footed policemen, then it's about time I resigned."

I had my own views on that subject, but did not give them. What I did do was to take him aside and tell him that for the next twelve hours he must not let Voss out of his sight.

"You had better carry a gun," I said.

He roared with laughter.

"If I see the gentleman who did the shooting, he will be sorry even if he carries two guns."

Which was all very fine and large, but didn't impress me.

He went into Voss' bedroom and closed the shutters. He had a camp bed brought, and as soon as Max Voss was inside the room he had the camp bed put right across the door.

A lot of people think I am brave, but I'm not. I was in a bit of a funk when I walked down to the Flash, even though I had two police officers with me, for I knew that somewhere lurking in the darkness was the man who had tried to kill Voss.

I was absolutely dead for want of sleep, but before I lay down I had several little jobs to do, and one of them was to go through the money I had found in Veddle's pocket, count it and seal it up ready to be sent to the Yard in the morning.

Counting that money took me longer than I had expected – it was two o'clock – because that money spoke and confirmed all that had come to me when the shot was fired.

At half-past two I lay down on the bed, but I could not sleep. Being over tired is almost as bad as not being tired at all. I lay there thinking about Veddle and John Field and the girl, Marjorie Venn, and she came into my thoughts more frequently than either of the other two.

Once I thought of getting up and making myself some tea, or pouring out something stronger, but I turned over again on the other side and tried to sleep.

As a matter of precaution I had planted my two men half-way between the house and Tadpole Copse. I don't know whether I am sorry or glad I did that.

I couldn't sleep. I was absolutely like a wet rag, and, getting up, I walked to the window. The dawn was beginning to break. There was just enough light to make shadows. I thought it was a tree in the middle of the lawn – a little tree I had overlooked – until I saw it move towards the water's edge.

"Who is that?" I shouted. "Stop, or I'll fire."

I didn't have a gun, but I thought the threat would be enough. Then I saw that it was a woman who was running towards the river, and my heart jumped, for I recognised the figure in the dawn light – it was Marjorie Venn!

I rushed out of the room, switching on the light as I went, and ran down the stairs. The front door leading to the lawn was wide open, so was the door of the study. When I got to the lawn I could see nothing. On the river's edge there was no sign of a boat.

I blew my whistle for the two men. Before they could come down I went back to the house and into the study. The safe door was wide open. The safe had contained a number of documents, and I could not see for the moment if any had been taken. Then, turning my head, I saw on the hearth a little bundle of ashes that was still smoking.

You know how paper burns: it leaves the letters all shiny and visible against the black background. I didn't need my glasses to know that the heap of ashes that was smouldering was the last will and testament of John Field, the will that had left all his money to Marjorie Venn.

I remembered it being in the safe. I remembered too that Marjorie had a key of the safe and a key of the front door.

By the time I finished my examination I heard my name called from the other side of the Flash. The two men had come down to the water's edge, and I ordered them to cross, as the motor-boat was on their side of the lake. They had seen nobody, heard nothing but my shout.

It was getting lighter and things were becoming visible. I was so certain that it was impossible to pick up the traces of Marjorie Venn that, having given the men some instructions, I went back to the study, lay down on the sofa and was asleep in a few minutes.

I suppose an old man does not require the amount of sleep that a youngster needs. The study clock was striking seven when I woke.

I had taken a big glass cover which was over a piece of native carved ivory and had put it over the ashes in the grate before I lay down. The nature of the document was as plain as the daylight that showed it. There was the will, and I wondered if a burnt will could be proved. But would Marjorie Venn want to prove it? I wondered for a few minutes whether it was she or the negress who had burned away a fortune. No – I couldn't have mistaken Marjorie.

Whilst the servants were getting breakfast I sat down at the table, took out some paper and wrote out the case as I saw it. That is a weakness of mine. I like to put A to B and B to C. In half-an-hour I had the whole of the case laid out as I understood it. Exactly what was the beginning of the trouble, and – to me – what was the end. It was not a very long document; it took me nine minutes to read to the chief constable (I got him out of his bed) and to receive my instructions from him.

Our chief constable is a very sensible man who trusts his subordinates, and apparently he did not send Gurly down, but Gurly had sent himself down on the promise that he would not interfere with me. Maybe the chief constable was lying when he said that, but it sounded true.

I finished the telephone talk, went up and had a bath and shaved. When I came down the two night watchers were on the lawn, waiting to be dismissed. If they expected me to put them to bed they were entitled to a grievance. I crossed the Flash with them and we went up to Mr Voss' house together.

He was an early riser, and his staff were usually up and about when most servants were thinking of turning over for their last little snooze. Even the butler was on his job.

"Mr Gurly is still asleep," he said.

"What time does Mr Voss wake up as a rule?" I asked.

He told me that he usually took in the early morning tea about eight o'clock when Mr Voss had a late night, and seven when he had an early one.

"I was bringing it up now," he said.

Gurly was snoring like a pig. I didn't kick him, because he was my superior. I merely made a few faces at him – that didn't harm anybody.

He took a long time to wake up.

"Hullo, Minter!" he growled. He was never at his brightest in the morning. "What's doing?"

I told him I had come to see Voss, and, getting up, he cleared away his bed.

"I haven't heard from him all night long," he said as I knocked at the door.

"He doesn't seem to hear us now," I said, and knocked again.

There was no reply.

I hammered on the panel, but still there was no answer. Peeping down through the keyhole, I saw that the key was still in the lock, and sent the butler to find a crowbar. I knew there was one hanging in a glass case with a fire hatchet farther along the corridor.

With the crowbar I forced the door open and walked in. The room was empty; the lights still burnt, and the closed curtains kept out whatever daylight there was. But the room was empty, and the bed had not been slept in. Max Voss had vanished as completely and as mysteriously as Marjorie Venn!

12

Pulling aside the curtains, I saw that the shutter was unfastened and that one of the windows was ajar. There was no ladder against the portico; I knew that, because I should have seen it when we came to the house.

Gurly was absolutely shaking with excitement.

"How did they get him away? He's a pretty heavy man to carry, and I heard no sound. Have a look at the balustrade – there'll probably be blood on it…"

He was firing off directions to the butler when I left him.

I had Voss' car brought round and went straight to Garry Thurston's house. I expected he would be up, and I wasn't disappointed. He was strolling on the lawn before the house, and he must have been out and about for some little time, for he was wearing tennis flannels, and told me as calmly as you please that he was cooling off after a set.

"Does Mrs Field play tennis?" I asked sharply, and he smiled.

"Mrs Field went to London last night," he said very deliberately, "and her son. She told me all I wanted to know. It wasn't very pleasant hearing for me, but then, I knew much worse before she came."

I sort of scowled at him.

"That sounds like chapter one of a thrilling detective story," I said.

"The last chapter," he answered. "I hope I haven't given you a lot of trouble, Mr Minter – I certainly didn't intend to. The fact is, I've had a perfectly dreadful few days, and I have been so engrossed in my own business that I haven't troubled very much about other people's feelings. How is Mr Voss?"

I didn't answer him.

"Is there anything you want to see me about?"

"Yes, there is," I said. "Young man, I warn you that I'm out for blood. I've no respect for you nor your manor house nor your money nor – "

"Anything that is thy neighbour's," he smiled. "I realise that, superintendent. I can help you up to a point, and tell you the truth up to a point. Beyond that I am afraid I cannot promise either to be helpful or veracious."

He pulled up two wicker chairs and, putting them facing each other, sat down in one of them. I didn't feel like sitting; besides, a man standing up has got an advantage when he's cross-examining a man who's sitting down. One of the best lawyers at the Bar told me that.

"Last night," I said, "Miss Marjorie Venn left her lodgings very hurriedly – "

"In a motor-car," said Garry Thurston coolly. "Somebody sent a note for her, and that somebody was me. I wanted to see her very, very particularly, and I had something to tell her which induced her to go away with me."

His frankness took my breath away.

"It was you who brought the car for her?"

He nodded.

"And took her to London?"

"No."

"Where did you take her?" I asked.

He looked towards the house.

"She's there – in fact, she has been there since last night."

"And she hasn't left the house all night?" I said sarcastically.

"As to that, I am not prepared to say," said Garry Thurston. "If she strolled with me in the night you may be sure she had a very good reason. She is not the sort of young lady who does things without a very good cause."

His cheek took my breath away.

"She's in the house – can I see her?"

He nodded.

"She's changing. We've been playing tennis all the morning."

"Have you been near Voss' house?" I asked.

He shook his head. "No."

"Do you know where Voss is at this moment, and who took him away?"

He looked at me steadily.

"I've told you all that I'm going to tell you," he said. "Fortunately, you cannot put me in a torture chamber; more fortunately still, I am a very rich and influential young man. Not," he added, "that that makes a great deal of difference to you, Sooper. When I say that I am paying you a compliment. But your immediate superiors are not going to make the mistake of prosecuting me unless they have a very excellent basis for their prosecution. I did not murder John Field or Veddle; I did not fire at you – I have an idea Veddle did that. In fact, I have done nothing for which the law can touch me."

I waited till he had finished, and then: "Are you quite sure about that, Mr Thurston?" I asked quietly. "Are you absolutely certain that in the past eight hours you have done nothing for which I can put you in the dock?"

He smiled again.

"Come along and have breakfast," he said, but I wasn't going to allow him to blarney me.

I wanted to see the young lady, and he made no objection. She came down into the big library a few minutes after I had seated myself.

Marjorie Venn was very pale, but I never saw a girl who was more composed or surer of herself. There was a look in her face that I had never seen before, a sort of – what's the word? Serenity, that's it – that made her like somebody new.

She gave me a little smile as she came in, and held out her hand. As I wasn't Gurly I took it.

"Now, young woman," I said, "will you explain why you came to my house in the middle of the night?"

"It was to be my house," she said, her lips twitching. "Yes, I'm not denying it, superintendent: I did come into the study, I did open the safe, and I did burn Mr Field's will."

"Why on earth?" I asked her.

"Because I didn't want the money. It belongs to his wife. It was her devotion which helped Field to find the mine. Every penny of it belongs to her and her child. It would have been easy to have accepted the will and to have handed the money and property to her," she went on, "but I didn't want my name associated with Mr Field in any way."

I didn't take my eyes off her.

"And so you prefer to be a poor woman?"

"Miss Venn will not be a poor woman," Garry broke in. "There are two reasons why she will not be, and one of them is that she and I are to be married next week."

I played my trump card.

"With your father's consent?" I asked her, and her colour changed.

"Yes," she said in a low voice, "with my father's consent."

Garry Thurston was looking at me. I felt his eyes searching my face, and I got a little kick out of the knowledge that I'd given him a bit of a shock.

And then I dropped all the friendly stuff and began to ask her questions. Any other girl would have been rattled, but she fenced with me so cleverly that at the end of half-an-hour I knew no more than I had at the beginning, and, what was worse, she hadn't given me a handle that would help me to force her to speak.

When I got back to Hainthorpe I found Gurly had collected half the Berkshire constabulary and had organised a grand search of the grounds.

"I'm looking for a well. There must be one in the park somewhere… A gardener told me that he'd heard there was such a thing."

"What do you want with a well?" I asked. "Have the taps gone dry?"

But he was the sort of man who must have a well and a dead body to round off any case in which he was engaged. I often think that

Gurly got most of his ideas of police work out of these sensational stories that are so popular nowadays.

I didn't trouble to look for the well, but put through a call supplementing the one I had sent from Garry Thurston's place. But I knew just how small my chance was, and I wasn't disappointed when by noon the County Police reported blank; but I knew London was working, that the ports were being watched, and that every train that drew out of town, or pulled into a seaport, was being combed for my man.

It was early in the afternoon that I got the message from the Bixton Cottage Hospital. Bixton lies on the river; it would be one of the healthiest places in England if it wasn't for the weir, which provides eighty per cent of the casualties that go into the red brick cottage which is called a hospital. That weir is a pretty dangerous spot even in daylight, and doubly dangerous to a man who's rowing for his life in the dark and tries to land in order to avoid observation from the lock.

When they took him out of the water he was so near dead that the policeman who had heard him shout and went in after him didn't think he was worth artificial resuscitation; but being an amateur, and having just passed through his first-aid course, he had a cut at it, and nobody was more surprised than he when he heard the drowned man breathing.

He didn't recover consciousness till round about lunch-time, and the first person's name he mentioned was Superintendent Minter.

They 'phoned me and I drove at top speed to the hospital. I had to wait for an hour, because the doctor wouldn't have him wakened, and I was taking tea with the matron when the nurse came for me, and I walked into the little ward and straight up to the bedside.

"Hullo, Wills!" I said.

Veddle's brother lay on the bed, looking more dead than alive. I could see he was frightened, and I knew why.

"You were a bit excited last night, weren't you?" I asked him. "That shot you fired at Voss wasn't any too good. You shouldn't have missed him."

He looked away.

"I didn't shoot at anybody," he said sullenly. "You can't prove that I shot at anybody."

And this was true. If I was going to get a story out of Wills I'd have to hold up on that shooting charge until he did a little confessional work, and I rather fancied he was too wide awake to tell me much.

He didn't seem inclined to say anything, and for a long time he just lay, avoiding my eyes and ignoring my questions. Then, suddenly: "You've got nothing on me, Sooper, except the disciplinary charge – did they give you my brother's statement? It was in my pocket – I don't think it's been thrown away. I've been carrying it ever since he handed it to me the other night. He knew something was going to happen, and he said he was taking no chances – he had the whole story written in case somebody got him, or they framed up a charge against him. It's written on the back of a calendar and one sheet's missing. But there's nothing against me in it, Sooper. You can talk about shooting as much as you like, and you can be as suspicious as you like, but you can prove nothing. I helped my brother because he's the only pal I ever had. I took the job down at Lone House not to protect Field but to find out something my brother wanted to know."

It was perfectly true, what Wills said: there was no evidence against him. We never found the gun he used when he shot at Voss; but in those loosely written pages that I read carefully that night I discovered the reason for the shooting.

13

I'm not giving you this document word for word. It was long, and a lot of Veddle's statements were wholly inaccurate.

Field and his partner, Venn (he afterwards called himself Voss) located a mine in Africa. Venn, who was married to a charming Colonial girl, sent her to England, where her child might be born, and the two partners continued their search. The mine was located through the instrumentality of a native chief, whose daughter Field married.

He tried also to secure from the chief, his father-in-law, a supply of raw gold that was in the village, and, when this was denied him, attacked the village, himself leading a hostile tribe. At the time Venn was living in the chief's hut, a very sick man. He cared very little what became of him. News had reached him that his wife had died in childbirth. He did not know then, or until many years afterwards, that the letter which came to him was written by Field, designed to drive a sick man to suicide.

Field went back to England, an immensely wealthy man, quite confident that his sometime partner had died in the forest. He did not take his black wife with him – she followed, with her child, and located him. She was missionary-trained, spoke good English. Even she did not know that Voss was alive.

He had wandered from one tribe to another, careless of his fate, and quite ignorant of the fact that his partner had found and was working the mine they had sought, or that the attack upon the village had been instigated by Field. He only discovered this when, as a comparatively wealthy trader, he returned to the old village and received from the dying chief a legacy which made him a very rich man – the major portion of that store of crude gold which Field had taken such risks to procure. For the risks were very real. He was working his mine under charter from the Congo Government, a charter which would have been instantly revoked if his share in the rebellion had been traced.

Without any very hard feeling against the man who had treated him shabbily, Venn came back to England, and again an accident revealed the truth. The letter he had received in the forest, telling him of his child's death, had been written by Field. Venn's wife had died in poverty a year before he arrived in England, and the child, he learned to his horror, was in Field's employment.

A property which was adjacent to Lone House was in the market, and Voss obviously sat down cold-bloodedly to plan the murder of the man who had allowed his wife to starve, and who now, for all he knew, had victimised Marjorie Venn. He must prepare his alibi in advance, and he appeared in the county as a man who had lost the use of his legs, could not move except in a mechanically propelled chair. He had the house altered, lifts installed, all the paraphernalia of infirmity were gathered, and the legend of the cripple who could not walk became very well known throughout the country.

He must have been something of an artist in his way. I have met men like that before, but Voss, or Venn, could give points to all of them. He reconnoitred the ground, decided exactly the dramatic manner in which his crime should be committed, and waited patiently for the right assistant to turn up.

Veddle was the man: an ex-convict, utterly dishonest, a man who read his employer's letters, and who, to Venn's consternation, surprised his secret. From that moment Veddle was doomed – from his statement it looked as though he was under the impression that his fortune was made.

Voss seized the opportunity to reveal his whole plan to his subordinate. It promised untold riches to this blackmailer – for Veddle had made another discovery, namely, that Marjorie Venn was his employer's daughter and would one day be a very rich woman. He kept his secret to himself, not even hinting to Voss that he knew as much, and in his clownish way he tried to make good with the young lady.

He had a grievance himself against Field, who had beaten him up, and he became the more willing to help his employer toward his revenge.

You will remember that Mr Voss always wore a peculiarly marked jacket and a white hat? On the day of the murder Veddle was waiting in the copse dressed exactly like his master. As the electric chair went into the wood it stopped, and the two men changed places. Veddle had received careful instructions – that was in the first clue I found. He was to go up the hill, stop at a certain bush, turn at a certain stone, so that he faced Amberley Church. In this position he would be visible for miles around. He would also have a commanding view of Tadpole Copse.

The moment he received the signal, he was to come down the hill in third speed. Voss had chosen his man well. Wills, the watching detective, had been got rid of through his brother. The moment the chair moved on, with Veddle in the seat, Voss threw off his check coat and slipped into the water, swimming across the Flash, and made his way over the lawn to the study.

He may have carried a knife; it is unlikely that he went without arms; but the Sword of Tuna was easy to grasp. Field must have had his back to him when he struck.

You must remember that Voss wore nothing but a bathing suit. He was in the water and across the Flash in a few minutes; he was a powerful swimmer. Arriving in Tadpole Copse, he found the smoke pistol that Veddle had ready in his overcoat pocket and fired his signal. The moment Veddle saw this, he brought his car down the hill and through the wood. Here Voss was waiting – I don't know whether to call him Voss or Venn. He had dried his head and face roughly with a towel, which he had pushed into a hollow tree, and with his check coat and dummy collar, and a rug over his knees, nobody would have dreamed that the man in the chair that came out of one end of the wood was not the man who went in at the other.

Almost immediately Veddle got into his long coat and hid his clothes and made for his cottage. The moment a hue and cry was raised it was necessary to get Veddle out of the way. Full arrangements had been made, but Veddle was not taking any risks. He refused to leave the same night, and hid himself in his cellar.

I don't know how he discovered that his employer was double-crossing him. I think it may have been the fact that I was at the house.

The moment the hue and cry was raised Veddle lost his nerve and bolted. I found his money – the money that Voss had supplied him with and which was to get him out of England. I've reason to believe that he was actually hiding at Hainthorpe, in the house itself. It was afterwards that he went back to the cottage and hid himself in the cellar.

Voss was in a difficulty: he had to find a new supply of money. I knew exactly what had happened when I counted the money we had found on the dead body of Veddle, for one of the notes was splattered with ink; it was the same note I had seen in the possession of Max Voss.

The mystery of the shooting in the night was never thoroughly cleared up. I am satisfied in my own mind that Veddle was the would-be assassin, and that, believing his employer was trying to double-cross him, he had shot at him through his bedroom window. I don't like to think that Max Voss fired at me in the copse, and worked out a fake attack upon himself, but even this is possible.

There was somebody who knew his secret. The one man in the world he did not wish to know – that was Garry Thurston. Garry had a telescope on his terrace, and on the afternoon that Veddle, disguised as his master, went to the top of Jollyboy Hill, Mr Garry Thurston took a look at him through his telescope and immediately recognised the servant.

He was distracted because he was fond of Voss. He could not betray him. He was, I believe, bewildered, and then he heard that Field had a negro wife and wheedled the address where she was staying out of one of my men and went in search of her. It was she who told him the story of the two partners and in a second he guessed that Marjorie Venn was Voss' daughter. He wanted to get her out of the way. He wanted still more to save the life of the girl's father. Whether he assisted him to escape I cannot prove – escape he did and was never seen again in England.

That he killed Veddle in cold blood I am sure. Veddle had got on to his brother by telephone and arranged that they should meet in Tadpole Copse. He packed his suitcase, went down into the wood, handed over the statement to his brother, who was all along suspected. Wills rowed back to the Thames, never doubting that his brother would follow.

Naturally Voss didn't want the Veddle case to get into the papers: he knew that Wills would be on his track.

A queer case, an unsatisfactory case. I always look upon a murder case as unsatisfactory when nobody is hanged. At the same time I should not have liked Max Voss to have taken the nine o'clock walk: he was a decent fellow as murderers go.

THE SOOPER SPEAKING

When people get short on topics of conversation they say to me: "Sooper, you ought to write a book." And I always say: "I got no time." Anyway, superintendents of police don't write books. They know too much. And besides, I can't spell. Never could. There was a woman down at Wembley who used to throw my uneducation in my face every time I pinched her husband. He *was* educated. Wrote five hands, all different. And there was a lady down in Kent who used to report me regular to the Chief Commissioner because I didn't say "my lady" to her — wife of a city sheriff or something. Anyway, she never asked me why I didn't write a book. She knew I was low.

In my young days police constables didn't have to do much more than read and write. The only etiquette they were supposed to know was never to give backchat to their superiors or argue with a man who threatened to punch 'em on the nose. But nowadays, when everybody's gone scientific and lots of policemen speak French, a chap like me would have no chance of promotion.

I got where I got on merit, as I was explaining to Mr Frank Dewsbury one night. I often tell people this, otherwise they wouldn't know, but would be thinking I got my promotion because the chief was sorry for me.

Mr Dewsbury is a man I respect very highly. Once upon a time I didn't respect him because he was a stockbroker and wasn't rich. I used to think he drank or abused other good habits, but apparently there was nothing wrong with him. He had a house in Elsmere Gardens, and some nights when I had nothing better to do I used to go in and have a chat with him. That's how I discovered he didn't drink – I'd take four whiskies to his two. So you might say he was almost a teetotaller. He was a tall young man, nearly as tall as me, a good looker, a bit of a boxer, and he was an officer in the Territorials. He had a high respect for me – in fact, he was as intelligent a young man as you could wish to meet.

But he wasn't rich. So far as I could discover, there are quite a lot of people on the Stock Exchange who haven't got a million. He was one of them. His uncle was Mr Elijah Larmer. I was sorry to hear this, because Larmer and I have never been boy friends. He is a man as old as me, but he hasn't worn as well.

Larmer owns most of West Kensington – land and estates to him are what back gardens are to me and you. He lives on the outskirts of my division in a big, dirty-looking house that is so surrounded by shrubs and trees that you can hardly see it from the roadway. Rich? That man could buy the Bank of England and still have enough money left to buy a lunch.

The first time I met him professionally was twelve years ago. He was the kind of man who liked to have a lot of ready money at his hand. I don't say that he distrusted banks, but in the estate agent's business, especially in his early days, most of the deals were done with ready money. He had a big strong-room built in his basement, and he often had as much as a hundred thousand pounds in that safe room of his. And naturally, being a mean old fellow, when he had that strong-room made he got the cheapest builder and the cheapest safe-maker and used cut price material.

Mean? He was so mean he used to count the pips in an orange. When they put the new heating into St Asaph's Church, he went twice a day to save his own gas.

As I say, I came into touch with him over this new strong-room of his. It was only a strong-room to a child with a wooden spade. When Harry Pinford went after it with a kit of tools it was the weakest strong-room you could imagine. They cut a hole through the strongest part of it one night and got away with eight thousand pounds.

"What are the police for?" he says to me (I was acting inspector at the time) when I went to see the job. "Are they ornaments? I pay rates and taxes to be protected. Look at that strong-room! Burgled under the nose of the police!"

I pointed out that it was under his own nose too. I showed him the rotten lock on the kitchen door and the cheap fastenings on the pantry window and the burglar alarm that didn't go off because he'd been too mean to keep the batteries in order. He reported me for impertinence and threatened to have me broken. He got so that he used to think I was responsible. I took Harry about three weeks afterwards, but he'd planted the money. Larmer was like a lunatic when he didn't get his eight thousand back. He had a new steel door fitted and new burglar alarms.

"My uncle," said Mr Dewsbury, "is difficult."

He was being very difficult with young Dewsbury, who was his uncle's broker. Larmer did quite a lot of speculating on the Stock Exchange and made money. And he had quite a number of friends who also did their business through Frank Dewsbury.

Frank was doing well when he met a girl, Miss Margaret Pinder, the daughter of a man who had once caught old Larmer over a law deal. Larmer didn't know anything about the engagement for a long time. When he did he sent for Frank.

"What's this dam' nonsense about the Pinder girl?" he said. "I'd sooner see you dead than married to the daughter of that old crook Joe Pinder."

"I'm very fond of her," said Frank. "In fact, I'd sooner be dead than not marry her. Be reasonable, Uncle Elijah – Betty is not responsible for her father's actions. Besides, he's dead."

"Naturally he's dead," snarled old Larmer, who had a working arrangement with the Almighty, "but his daughter's alive! Didn't Joe Pinder play the dirtiest trick on me? Wasn't he a crooked-minded twister…" And so forth and so on.

I happened to drop in to dinner the night after. There was Frank pretending not to care, and there was Betty, a very pretty, straight backed girl who wasn't crying over the business but was looking rather serious. There was a sort of aunt there too. She spoke at intervals, saying the things she'd like to do to Mr Larmer. Most of 'em were strictly illegal.

"He's taking his business away from me, and I suppose his friends will do the same," said Frank. "He's also cutting me out of his will – "

"That doesn't mean a lot," said Betty. "He told you he was only leaving you a thousand pounds – all his money is going to mental hospitals."

"If I had my way with him," said the aunt, who was a God-fearing woman who wore a gold cross round her neck and a copper cross on her waist, "I'd boil him in oil. A man like that doesn't deserve to live."

She was Betty's aunt.

I've naturally got a very soft place for young people. They want all the sympathy that we old chaps can give 'em. They're so darned foolish. I never see a young man that I don't think of him as an oyster who's mislaid his shell. At the same time, I never thought I should lower myself to be sorry for a stockbroker. He was a good soldier – he was in the war at sixteen – and a good amateur theatrical player, and they tell me the way he handled a tennis racket would make Lenglen look like Cousin Jane from the country. But I doubt if he was a good stockbroker. I don't know what kind of brain you've got to have to be a good stockbroker, but he hadn't got it. I knew that the minute he told me he wasn't a millionaire.

I didn't see him again for nearly a month, but I heard through my sergeant, who wastes time picking up items about honest people that he ought to be using in the pursuit of his duty, that young Mr Dewsbury was having a bad time.

My sergeant – it was Martin at the time – got very friendly with Mr Dewsbury and used to call in every other night – not that that meant anything: he'd go almost anywhere for a free drink.

"He knows quite a lot about police work," Martin told me. "I've never seen a man so interested – I think he's going to write a book."

About a week after this I saw Mr Dewsbury and Martin up west. It was the sergeant's night off, and he could do pretty well as he liked, but I was kind of curious. I am one of those old-fashioned detectives that can't deduce anything. If I see a man opening a window with a jemmy in the middle of the night, I deduce that he's a burglar, and if he shows fight on the way to the station I get a sort of deduction that he wants clubbing. I used to carry a small rubber truncheon in my right hip pocket, and it's been a good friend of mine. But working out the colour of a man's eyes from the cigar ash he's left on the library carpet has never been a hobby of mine. That's scientific and educated, and I'm neither.

So I didn't start deducing about him and Dewsbury being college chums, but I just started asking, which I've always found is the best way of getting information. It appeared that Dewsbury was very anxious to see some of the underworld. There's a special brand of underworld round the Tottenham Court Road that's just there to be seen. It doesn't mean anything, and whenever I show visitors round and take 'em to this exhibition, I always feel as though I'm deceiving innocent children. It's like being asked to take a man to see the dangerous snakes at the Zoo and showing him the lizard house.

"But he knows as much about the game as I do," said Martin.

"Which isn't much," said I; for a senior officer should never lose an opportunity of keeping a young detective in his place. Vanity is the curse of the service.

"Soho didn't mean anything to him, so I took him along to the Grands and let him take a look at one or two of the boys. And, Sooper, Jim Mosker is in town – he slipped out as I went into the bar, but I saw him."

Now, where Jim Mosker is, "Dowsy" Lightfoot is, and naturally all my interest in Mr Dewsbury's first course in criminal jurisprudence got off the car and made way for Jim and his snaky friend.

Jim Mosker was one of the cleverest safe-blowers in Europe: a nice, quiet-spoken man, who could prove an alibi in three languages. He hadn't been in town for I don't know how long. Jim wasn't one of these vulgar, haphazard burglars that only go after the stuff when they're short of money and generally get caught with the goods because they haven't taken the trouble to reconnoitre the ground. Jim went after the big money in a big way. He'd take a year to prepare, and preparation with Jim meant the last button on the last gaiter, as Napoleon said. If it wasn't Napoleon it was Bismarck.

Before Jim Mosker did the actual work he knew the Christian names and family history of every clerk, cashier, messenger and office boy at the bank – he generally worked banks. He knew just what the manager's private trouble was, her name and what worried her.

His partner was another kind. "Dowsy" Lightfoot supplied any violence that the combination required. He had no conscience, no pity and no eyelashes. He was a pale, hairless man without feeling.

At the earliest opportunity I looked up Jim and found him at the Grands, which is a sort of high-class club for low-class people. It was run by Wilkie Meed, an old-time boxer, and it was very well conducted, for Wilkie still packed a punch that hurt. In a way it was rather a healthy sort of place: you never saw funny people there, and a fellow who strolled in one night and asked for a shot of dope was taken to the hospital under the impression he'd had it. Just honest-to-God thieves, confidence men, screw-men, but always the elite of the profession.

I found Jim sitting at a corner table in the big bar, and of course that clever sergeant of mine was all wrong when he said that Jim thought he had missed being seen.

"How are you, Sooper?" said Jim, getting up and shaking me by the hand. "Sit down and have a drink." And when the waiter had come over, he said: "Vermouth, with just two drops of absinthe and a little water."

And mind you, he hadn't seen me for six years. What a memory!

"I saw a fellow here the other night: they tell me he's your sergeant, Martin. I didn't like to talk to him because he had a friend of mine with him."

"How's Dowsy?" I asked, for there was no sign of the snake man.

Jim smiled. He was a chubby little man who wore rimless glasses.

"Dowsy? He's coming over tomorrow night. I'm getting rather tired of Paris, Sooper. This is the good little town, only you people won't leave me alone. All the time you think I am doing something unlawful."

He went on in this way for a long time, and I let him have his spiel. I knew he'd been in France and Berlin, but he was not on the books and it was no business of mine to connect him with that big jewel robbery in Friedrichstrasse or an unpleasant little affair in Lyons.

"What's this joke about the gentleman who was with Martin being a friend of yours?" I asked.

Jim smiled quickly.

"He's a man named Dewsbury. I met him three months ago in Paris. A very nice fellow." He shrugged his shoulders. "I don't care two hoots whether he knows my sad story or not," he said, "but it might hurt his feelings if he had a heart-to-heart talk with you and heard I was a naughty boy. Not that I am," said Jim. "I'm spending what you would describe as my declining years regretting my foolish past. Thanks to a legacy which my aunt left me – "

"Let's keep to facts, Jim," I said. "Where did you meet this Mr Dewsbury?"

He'd met him at a big restaurant just off the Bois. Somebody introduced him, and they had driven out in Jim's car to Enghien and had a little gamble at the tables.

"It was a very mild affair," said Jim, "and there was no private seance afterwards. No, I liked the lad; there's something very straightforward and English about him."

Which was Jim's way of saying that he thought Frank Dewsbury was a fool.

Now I knew Jim's method as well as I know the road to Clapham Common. That wasn't an accidental meeting in Paris. Jim was after big money – he'd never come to England unless.

After we'd had a couple of drinks Jim began to get truthful and surprising.

"I don't know why I lie to you, Sooper," he said, in his frank, boyish way, "but here's the whole strength of Dewsbury and how we met him. It was in a restaurant, but nobody introduced us. Dowsy had had four drinks and was full of danger. When we got to the restaurant we found Dewsbury sitting at our table. We were so late that the head waiter had handed over our park and told him he could sit there. And then Dowsy got a bit unpleasant and whipped in a quick one. It wasn't quick enough for this Dewsbury man, who ducked and landed Dowsy a short-arm jab under the heart that laid him out. Naturally enough, when the tumult and the shouting died, we got together like brothers, and that's how we come to meet him. And that's a fact. Of course, the head waiter said he didn't put Dewsbury at our table at all, but he'd just sat down and wouldn't be moved. The whole proceedings were very queer."

I knew Mr Dewsbury often went to Paris. He had a great friend there, an estate agent who did a lot of business with old Larmer, his uncle. Just about then, trade was brisk, for some of the Russian nobility who had saved a bit of money were buying estates in England. Dewsbury told me this when I saw him the next night.

He was very cheerful except that he spoke about his uncle and Betty Pinder. He had already bought a house at Purley when old man Larmer came.

"The moral is, Sooper," he said, with a little laugh, "never count your wedding presents till after the wedding!"

He told me his business had dropped to nothing, and that every time he met Elijah, as he frequently did, the old man got him by the buttonhole and told him a new one against Joe Pinder.

"I should hate to hang for Uncle Elijah," he said.

I asked him where he got his interest in crime, and he took me by the arm and led me back to his house. I'd never examined his library before, and I was surprised to find the number of books he had on the subject – almost as many as that bird I got hung over the Big Foot murder.

He told me that when he was in the trenches during the war he read nothing else, and he proved that he wasn't talking stuff when he told me the full history of Jim Mosker.

"Oh, yes, I knew them the moment I spotted them in Paris. I liked Jim, but the skinned one – ugh!"

I was interested. I was terribly interested.

"You didn't by any chance sit down at that table knowing they were coming and that Dowsy would start something?" I asked.

"Maybe I did," said Mr Frank Dewsbury very carelessly. "I thought it was a good way of getting acquainted. I tried the Sullivans first, but they're half-wits. Jim Mosker's got brains."

I didn't ask him why he tried to get acquainted with the Sullivans, who are just second-class thieves in the take-it-as-you-find-it class.

I'd already reported Mosker's presence in my district. He came twice to see Dewsbury. Miss Pinder evidently heard about it, because she called at my lodgings one night.

"You're a great friend of Frank's, aren't you? And I'm a little worried, Superintendent. Frank is the dearest fellow in the world, but he's awfully generous and broad-minded, and I've got a feeling that it isn't good for him to be seen about with Mr Mosker."

"You've met Mosker?" I asked.

She nodded.

"Yes; I don't like him. I don't know why: he's very nice and polite, but there's something about him…"

I didn't give her any biographical details. I thought it best to let Mr Frank Dewsbury do his own excusing.

"You see, Superintendent, what worries me so much is that just now Frank is awfully pinched for money. And knowing how desperate things are with him, I don't like to feel he's keeping bad company. He missed two engagements with me last week to dine with Mr Mosker."

I soothed her down, but I was a bit puzzled. Frank Dewsbury was not the kind of fellow that'll get so desperate that he'd take a corner with a man like Mosker. On the morning of the 18th of June – that was a few days after I'd spoken with the young lady – Frank Dewsbury asked me if I could see him. I told him to come down to the station, because I was pretty busy, and he arrived in a car packed full of baggage.

He had a little country bungalow within a couple of miles of the sea, and he was going there to write the opening chapters of a book on crime, and he wanted a few facts about the organisation of Scotland Yard. It was the first time I'd heard there was any. It's not for me to knock my superiors, so I did my best to give him a good impression. I saw him off, and at about five o'clock that afternoon we got a trunk call through from his cottage, asking me how London was cut up for police purposes. When I say "he asked me," I was out, but Martin, who is a rare talker, supplied him with all the information he wanted and more.

I didn't know, because old man Larmer didn't notify us, that at half-past three that afternoon a M Lacoste arrived from Paris with twenty-four million francs. They were in twelve packages, each containing two thousand mille notes, and M Lacoste was accompanied by a couple of armed guards. He drove from Victoria to the old man's house, where Elijah and his lawyer were waiting to complete a big land deal. They had a glass of grocery wine together, the old man put the money in his new strong-room, and the Frenchman and the lawyer drove away together.

Nobody had seen Jim Mosker or his pal, but nothing is more certain than that they were on the spot and that the party had been watched all the way from Paris to Mr Larmer's place.

This house stood on an island site; most of the grounds were in front, and behind was a mews containing about eight garages called Steverny Mews. Above each garage was a little flat intended for the chauffeurs, but the old man had turned out all his tenants months before and was converting these garages into flats for artistic people. As everybody knows, artistic people would rather live in a converted stable provided the roofs were low and the stairs were ladders, than they'd stay at the Ritz-Carlton. That's why they're artistic.

He had a garage of his own but he had dismissed his chauffeur and sent his car to a local garage proprietor. At half-past nine that night a big limousine came to the mews, the driver got down and, unlocking the door of Elijah's garage, drove the car in, and the gates were closed behind them. This was seen by a policeman who was standing at the end of the mews. It was a dark night and raining a little, and the policeman thought no more than that it was the old man's car.

A quarter of an hour later a tall policeman called at the front door.

"I've come from the Superintendent. He says he hears you've got a lot of money in the house: would you like me inside, sir, or outside?"

Larmer didn't like me, but I guess he was pretty well relieved to see this tall policeman – did I tell you that Dowsy Lightfoot stood six feet two inches in his socks?

"I'm not going to pay any police charges," he said, that being the first thought that occurred to him, but the policeman said there was nothing to pay and that it was a part of police duty, so Larmer let him stay in the kitchen.

Soon after there came a 'phone call from M Lacoste. It was very important: could Larmer come at once as the deal might have to be cancelled? This touched him on his tender spot. Having the policeman in the house made all the difference, and he went out, first placing the policeman in the little passage that led to the strong-room. Naturally enough, when he got to the Ritz-Carlton he was met by a very nice young man who said that Lacoste had gone out to see the Governor of the Bank of England, and he sat the old boy down in the lounge and told him the story of his life.

I heard about the robbery at midnight. At three o'clock in the morning we found Mosker; he was lying on the side of the Chiselhurst Road amongst the grass, and Dowsy was lying on the other. They were both handcuffed, and Dowsy was fit for hospital because, as he told me later, he'd had a beating up that he'd remember all the days of his life.

"No, I haven't got the stuff," said Mosker, when I interviewed him at the local police station. "I've been doubled, Sooper."

He then told me what had happened. The car they used for the job was a fast old limousine, one of the kind that has a luggage space on top and a sheet of mackintosh to keep the baggage dry. They had faked the car so as to look as though it were going on a week-end trip, with cardboard boxes under the waterproof. Jim Mosker was the driver; he went straight into the garage, locked the door, and waited till Dowsy was planted in the house. Once they got rid of old man Larmer, the rest was easy. They cut into the strong-room with the kit that Mosker had brought in the car, got the money, threw it into the limousine, and were out of the house long before the young man who was entertaining Mr Larmer had got to the place where he was vaccinated.

"We went straight for the coast I'd arranged for a tug to take us across to Dunkirk," said Jim, "and it looked easy once we shook London astern. We'd got to a lonely sort of common; I don't know the place – Chiselhurst, was it? – when I saw a leg come over the side of the car, and I realised that we'd been carrying a passenger on top under the tarpaulin. How he got there I don't know. He must have got into the garage whilst we were operating, but that doesn't matter.

"Before I could open my mouth be was standing on the running-board, and he pushed a gun under my armpit.

"'Stop,' he said. I couldn't see his face, but I could feel the pistol, and thought it best to stop, so I did. The light from the front lamps reflected back from the bushes, and the only thing I could see was that he had a half mask over the top of his face and a black moustache. Until then I thought he was just ordinary police. 'Step down and step lively,' he said, so I did. But Dowsy, who has never yet realised the inevitable, took a running kick at him. I don't know what he did to Dowsy – my poor pal just disappeared, and I didn't see him again till this feller hauled him out of the ditch and put the irons on him. By this time he'd got 'em on me, and Dowsy and I had to sit and watch our good earnings being dumped into a bag. Not that Dowsy saw much – he just laid there and groaned. I don't know what this feller hit him with but I think it had iron in it. That's all I can tell you, Sooper. I wouldn't have told you so much, if you hadn't found our tools in the car."

"You don't know who the man was who robbed you?" I asked.

Mosker shook his head.

"No. It's a bit hard, Sooper. And after the trouble we took to find out all that young Dewsbury knew!"

It struck me at the time that young Dewsbury might have been doing a little inquiry work himself.

I made a trip to where the car was found, and, examining the road about a hundred yards farther along, I saw wheel marks: the diamond-pattern tyre of a light car. But there was no trace of the third man, and that afternoon I drove on to see young Dewsbury. I thought, being an expert on crime, he might give me a theory. Besides which, I wanted to have a look at the tyres of his car.

I found him working away very cheerfully, though be didn't seem to have written much. I think he'd been changing his tyres all morning...

I make no accusations against any man. I harbour no unkind thoughts. All I know is that when Mr Frank Dewsbury was married he went away in his own Rolls. And he's gone back to stockbroking. I think he's found out how to deal with money. And how to get it.

CLUES

I've got a smart Aleck of a detective-sergeant in my division who is strong for clues. The harder they are the better he likes 'em. He reckons finger-prints are too childishly easy for a full-grown officer of the CID.

"I believe there is a lot in that tobacco-ash theory, Sooper," he said. "It's fiction, I know – but there's a lot of truth in stories."

So I put up to him the well-known case of the State against Uriah – or, better still, Uriah against David with Bathsheba intervening.

The chief was saying the other day that there has been nothing new in murder crime since the celebrated Cain and Abel affair.

"In fact, Sooper," he said, "you can dig down into the Old Book and find parallels for most every case that comes up at the Old Bailey."

Which, in a way, is true. All the same, crime was a mighty simple affair round about BC 3000. If a feller didn't like another feller he just dropped him down a well or snicked off his head, and what happened to the snicker depended on the kind of a pull he had with the chief priest or the king or whoever was the man on top.

There wasn't any come-back with Uriah, for instance, and no complications. They just handed him up to the front line trenches and sent him out single-handed to see what the Amalekites were thinking up for tomorrow's battle.

But if Uriah had had a tough brother Bill or a sister named Lou, there would surely have been trouble for David, and worse still if Uriah, instead of getting himself carved up by the enemy, had sneaked back to Headquarters by a roundabout way.

The David I'm thinking of was a mean man named Mr Penderbury Jonnes, who owned three stores on Oxford Street and had a country mansion near Hertford, to say nothing of a flat in Hanover Square. I happened to know Pen Jonnes. He was a Welshman on the soft goods side of the race. A tall, red-faced fellow with eyes like a puppy dog's and a moustache like a cavalry officer. He used to think that he was a bachelor in the sense that he hadn't any regular matrimonial arrangement. But this wasn't so.

He had a wife, though nobody seemed to have met her. She had been a shop-girl in one of his stores and he didn't find out until it was too late that her brother was Yorkshire Harry, the only cruiser-weight that ever went ten rounds with that Yankee fellow who held the title till some girl told him he looked grand in a dress suit.

Yorkshire Harry used to do a little blackmailing on the side, and he ran with the Stiney's, who were cracksmen on the top scale. Anyway, Penderbury took the shortest way out of trouble and was married at the Henrietta Street Registry Office. I expect he was sorry, because Yorkshire Harry was caught the very next year and died in Gloucester Gaol from some fool thing.

I used to get a whole lot of anonymous letters about Penderbury – written in a woman's hand. Every second word was spelt wrong. Generally the letters had a Hertford postmark, and if half the things they accused Jonnes of doing were true, he'd have lived permanently in jail.

It was then I found out about Mrs Jonnes and got a specimen of her handwriting. After that we didn't take too much notice of the anonymous letters, whether they were signed "A Frend" or "A lovver of Justise." Interfering between man and wife is the very last instruction in the police code. I gathered that Mrs Jonnes did not like her husband and let it go at that.

One letter I remember very well – I'll spell it according to my ideas of how it ought to be spelt.

"If he wasn't afraid that the police would come after him, why does he keep all that money in his safe ready in case he has to jump out of the country?"

As a matter of fact, I did know that Penderbury kept a lot of money in his safe at Hertford, and so did somebody else. Two burglars tried to "bust" the house once and it came out at the trial. As the judge says, "This is not a court of morality," and people can do pretty well anything they like so long as they don't obstruct the police in the execution of their duty or drive a car without a licence.

Jonnes had a cashier named Banford – Horace Angel Banford. I never quite got the hang of that "Angel" and I never asked him, though I knew him pretty well. He was one of those Adam's apple tenors who sang so well that nothing could improve him. People used to say what a pity it was that he didn't go to a master for a few lessons. He was that kind of vocalist But he went fine at our police orphanage concerts, and that is where I came to meet him. He was a tall, thin, sandy man with hollow cheeks, short sight and a schoolgirl complexion, and the last idea that he'd start was that he'd ever qualify for that 9 am walk from cell to gallows.

Crime and music were his hobbies. I was surprised, when he invited me down to his little flat in Bloomsbury, to find the number of books he had about criminals. But he was sensible with it – never thought he could spot a homicide by the colour of his eyes and the curious way he wagged his ears. One thing he was certain about.

"Nine out of every ten murderers wouldn't be caught if they weren't boneheads," he said to me one night. "A crime is like any other job. You've got to be efficient to hold it down."

We were all alone because his wife was out. She went out a lot – she was a great dancer.

"She goes with a lady friend," said Mr Banford. "Personally, dancing bores me, but she loves it,"

That made it all right. Anything Dora Banford loved – dress, dancing, pretty little jewels – was all right. Banford's salary was ten pounds a week – that's about fifty dollars American, isn't it? And he did everything on that – Bloomsbury flat, a well-dressed wife, jewels and dances.

And it can't be done.

I went again, because he had a book on the Leamington murder which he'd lent and was getting back, and naturally, as I was the man who pinched Pike Gurney, I wanted to see if the feller that wrote the book had given me all the credit I deserved.

I met Mrs Banford in the hall: she was pulling on her gloves when I went in, and I can tell you she was a peach. One of those fluffy little things with wild golden hair that never stays put. She sort of gave me a look under her long lashes and said (not out loud, but my receptivity is pretty good), "Who is the old bird with the big feet?" or something equally interesting.

Horace Angel fussed around her like a nanny before a baby's first party. He sort of leant over her and fanned her with his wings. Down to the street door he went with her, got her a cab and put her inside, and then he came back with his silly, thin face all red and smirky.

"The best wife in the world!" he said.

I was with him for two hours and picked out all the bits in the book about me. I must say that the fellow in the book was an honest man and only made one mistake. He said I took Pike as he was going into the Branscombe House Hotel, when in fact I took him as he was coming out.

At one o'clock the next morning I had a pressing engagement with the reserves. We raided the Highlow Club in Fitzroy Square. We had information that Fogini, the manager, was selling booze out of hours and that everybody who went to the Highlow didn't go to dance. There was a baccarat game on the top floor, and there were all sorts of nice little private dining-rooms where people stayed who didn't play cards and weren't keen on dancing.

The raid went according to plan, and in Room 7 I found Mrs Banford and Mr Jonnes. They were sitting at a little table with a very large bottle of champagne, and as far as I could see when I opened the door, he was holding her two hands across the table. She snatched them away when I barged in, and I saw a puzzled sort of look walking alongside her fear – she was trying to place me.

Jonnes went redder than usual.

"What the devil is the idea of this?" he snapped.

"You're under arrest," said I, "for consuming spirituous liquor after the hours by law prescribed."

Which is the classy way of saying that he was boozing out of hours. That made his colour run.

"Can't this be squared?" he said. "I'm Mr Jonnes, of Jonnes Mantle Corporation."

He yanked out his pocket-book.

"Don't insult me with five," I said, when he slipped a note. "My price is ten millions. Who is the lady?"

Of course I knew, but I didn't let on. He seemed to have forgotten all about her.

"Oh – " he said, like a man who had to bring his mind down to trifles, "she's Mrs Smith – an Australian lady."

I ordered him down to the dance room, where my boys were doing a little asking, and he went. This Mrs Banford's face was the colour of chalk and she was going after him when I called her back.

"I'm playing favourites for the first time in years," I said. "There's a pretty good fire escape at the back – I'll show you the way."

I did more than that, I took her down and tipped off the man on duty to let her pass out; said she was a Highness and we didn't want any Highnesses in this kind of scandal.

Jonnes came up next morning before the Marylebone magistrates and got his fine, and so far as I was concerned there was the end of the lady who went dancing with a girl friend.

Only things don't work out that way in life, which is a story that's continued an' continued.

About six months after this I stepped into the charge room at Limber Street Station, and what did I see? Horace Angel in the steel pen. He had the colour of a man who wasn't expected to live. Poor old Horace, caught with the goods. Two thousand pounds' worth of embezzlement on his soul. And there, resting his arm on the sergeant's desk, was Jonnes.

Horace Angel had nothing to say, and if he had he was short on speech. The jailer put him below and I strolled up to Penderbury Jonnes.

"He has been swindling me for years. I hate doing this, because I know his wife, poor little woman… But I trusted him. Why, I've even sent him down to Hertford with the key of my safe, where there are thousands of pounds…"

That was his end of it. When I interviewed Horace Angel in his dugout he gave me another slant to the story. It wasn't easy to get it, I can tell you, because when he wasn't weeping he was cursing Dora Banford and Penderbury Jonnes, and when he wasn't cursing Dora he was forgiving her, though I didn't notice that he forgave Penderbury much.

"We're going to start fresh when I come out," he said. "I never gave the little girl a chance, Sooper. All I wanted to do was read an' sing, and that's pretty dull for a woman. I've been a scoundrel and dragged her name in the mud. How that hound caught me I don't know – somebody on the inside must have seen the duplicate set of books – "

"Where did you make them up?" I asked.

"At home," he gulped. "God, what a fool I was! And they came straight to my flat and found them, Sooper. The hired girl must have been in their pay."

I let him go on.

"What's all this about Jonnes and your wife?" I asked.

"Nothing!" he said, very loud, but by-and-by I got it out of him.

Horace Angel had a friend who took a part in a west-end revue. This friend was a genuine tenor and had a couple of Come-my-love-the-moon-is-shining numbers. The queer thing about a stage tenor is that his throat is always going wonky. Just before the curtain goes up he strolls into the manager's office and says: "Sorry, old boy, but you'll have to put on the understudy," and naturally that leads to his having a lot of fuss made over him both before and after. But sometimes his throat does really go wrong, and Horace Angel, being a sort of floating understudy, was sometimes sent for to take his place.

One night a hurry-up call came to him – it was just after his wife had gone out to meet her girl friend – and Horace Angel went down to the theatre and made up. He was rather glad she had gone because she knew nothing about his understudying – Horace Angel was a little sensitive on the point of his voice.

His entry was towards the end of the first act. He was half-way through that love and moon stuff when he happened to look into the stage box. And there was Dora and Mr Jonnes. They were right at the back of the box and he gathered that they weren't interested in the play.

He got through the numbers and went home. There was a row, I suppose – he didn't tell me anything about that. And a few weeks later Jonnes pinched him.

Now whether Jonnes knew all the time that poor old Horace Angel was robbing him, and kept quiet because of the pull it gave him, or whether the auditors made the discovery, I've never found out.

At the Old Bailey the judge took a serious view of the crime and sent Banford down for three years. Two days after he was sentenced, Mrs Banford paid the rent in advance, locked up the flat, and went to Paris. Mr Jonnes followed the next day.

I had a talk with Uriah at Wormwood Scrubbs.

"There is only one way to hurt Jonnes," he said, "and when I come out I'm going to do it."

You don't take much notice of what newly convicted people say, and I passed it. I said nothing about Mrs Bathsheba except to lie up a message from her to say that she was bearing her affliction patiently. But he got to know when he was in Dartmoor. Every man has a friend who thinks that bad news is the only news worth knowing, and Horace Angel had several friends like that.

He said nothing; gave no trouble, went out of his cell at eight in the morning and had the key turned on him at four in the afternoon; sewed mail-bags, helped with the laundry and sang solos in the prison choir; and nobody guessed how Horace Angel's mind was slipping back to Lombroso and Mantazinni and his little crime library.

I never saw Jonnes and Dora together – not that I had many opportunities, but I never did. One of our inspectors who went over to bring back a bank clerk who had left London hurriedly with a block of the bank's assets, told me that she had a flat in the Avenue Bois de Boulogne (which is going some) but personally I knew nothing about her. But just about then I met Mrs Jonnes. The anonymous letters were piling up at the office and the chief was getting a little tired of reading 'em.

"Go down and see this Mrs Jonnes, Sooper, and tell her from me that until we get short on regular crime, we haven't time to investigate the chicken-chasing propensities of the modern husband."

I went down to Hertford midweek, because Mr Jonnes would be in town, and after a lot of difficulty I saw his wife. She had been a good looker, but years of Penderbury had sort of put an A in her face; if you've seen the nose lines and the drooping mouth of dissatisfied ladies you'll know what I mean. She had a Cockney accent with a sort of whistle in it, and what she didn't say about Mr Jonnes was that he was a perfect gentleman and a model husband.

"I live the life of a dog," she said. "One of these days I'll poison him – I will! If my poor darling brother was alive…!"

I got in a word or two about anonymous letters and she gave me her views on the police and the way they allowed wives to be beaten and locked up in rooms without food and treated like dirt by the servants.

"One of these days…!"

Those were her last words to me, and somehow I didn't feel that they were quite idle, for in Mrs Jonnes' veins ran the blood of three tough generations on both sides of the family.

When Horace was released I made it my business to call on him. He was sitting in the dining-room of the flat going through a lot of letters that had come during his absence. I remember that one of them had a cheque for his performance the night he peeked into the stage box.

"I'm starting all over again, Sooper," he said, and he was very cheerful. "A friend of mine has offered me a job in Peckham – not a big salary but enough to carry on with."

He did not mention his wife but he did speak of Jonnes.

"There is a man who ought to be out of the world," he said, as calmly as though he was talking about rice pie. "The more one thinks about Jonnes the more useless a creature he seems. He has never done a stroke of work for the money he has. His father left him the stores and he uses his wealth to corrupt the pure and the foolish."

"Quite a lot of people ought to be out of the world, Horace Angel," I said, "and sooner or later they will be. Give nature a chance and she'll put everybody where they belong."

He smiled at this: a sour, crooked smile.

This was a Thursday afternoon. On Saturday afternoon at four o'clock, Penderbury Jonnes went out of his big house at Hertford with a gun under his arm. He said that he was going to shoot rabbits. "Field Towers" – which was the name of his house – stands in about eighty acres of good rough shooting. The estate is surrounded by a wall except for about three hundred yards, where a bean-shaped covert of beech and pine trees separates his land from Lord Forlmby's estate. At about 5.35 one of Lord Forlmby's gamekeepers, stalking a stoat, came through the covert and saw a man lying huddled up on the ground. He ran across the rough and saw that it was Penderbury Jonnes and that he was dead. He had been shot at close range through the right shoulder, and his gun was lying by his side.

The gamekeeper sent for the police, and just about that time I had taken over the duties of chief detective inspector in the absence on leave of Joe Frawlett. There are four chief inspectors attached to Scotland Yard, and these men have the four districts of London, so that when the Hertford police asked for assistance it was my job to go down.

I got to the Towers about nine o'clock that night. It was dark and raining, but on the advice of the local police the body hadn't been moved, and a ring of space had been kept clear around the hurdles which had been put up over the body.

"The man must have been killed by a discharge of the gun," the doctor told me. "Though the wound is a very slight one. Probably a stray pellet reached his heart. One barrel of the gun has been fired, and the servants at the Towers say that they heard only one explosion."

The gun had been carefully wrapped in oiled silk and taken to the house to be photographed for fingerprints. I had a talk with the Chief Constable of Hertford, who was on the spot.

"The shot was fired at about 4.15," he said; "the only person seen near the spot was a motor-cyclist who was sheltering from the rain under a hedge on Lord Forlmby's side of the plantation. And the only discovery we have made is this glove."

He took it out of his pocket – a cheap cotton glove, right hand, slightly stained with mud and very damp.

"We found this at the end of the plantation," said the CC. "It was too dark to look for footprints and there is no other clue."

I told three of the Hertford police to make a search of the copse by hand-lamp, and then went up to the house to see Mrs Jonnes, and here I had my first shock.

She had left the Towers at some time in the afternoon.

"They'd been quarrelling all morning," said the butler; "the worst shindy I've ever heard!"

"Where did you see her last?" I asked.

"Going into the gun-room," he said.

I make a search of the gun-room. Jonnes was a methodical sort of a man, who had little ivory labels on every stand showing the maker and date of purchase of every piece. And there were two blank spaces. One was the home of the gun that had been found by Jonnes' side, the other a new gun bought a week before.

I went up into Mrs Jonnes' room. The wardrobe door was open, but there had been no attempt to pack anything. I made further inquiries. Jonnes' two-seated car was gone – had been taken out of the garage some time between four and six.

I inspected the other rooms, and in one on the ground floor, which Jonnes used as a study, I saw the safe. The butler, who was beginning to get more at home with the police, and had lost the feeling that any word he uttered might hang him, became a little more chatty.

"The row was about a woman named Banford. He was throwing her in Mrs Jonnes' face, saying how wonderful she was. Mrs Jonnes went almost mad…she was a very jealous woman."

About now the policemen I had sent to search the wood came back. They had made two finds. A rain-sodden sheet of newspaper in which something had been wrapped, and a small wooden box that somebody had hidden under a holly bush. The newspaper was a week-old copy of the *Echo de Paris*. The box was locked, but there wasn't much trouble in opening it. As a burglar kit it wasn't of much account. A couple of chisels, a jemmy, an electric torch, a key wrapped in tissue paper, a glazier's diamond and a folded square of fly-paper to hold a window pane when it was cut.

"That explains the glove," I said. "He carried them in his pocket to avoid finger-printing – but who goes travelling around with the *Echo de Paris*?"

The key interested me. I tried it on the safe and it opened the door.

There was one man to see, and that was Horace Angel. By twelve o'clock I was ringing the bell of his flat. I was a little surprised when he opened the door to me. He was dressed in an old suit and a pair of slippers, but before the fire was a pair of wet boots, and over the back of a chair was hung a pair of trousers that were wet to the knees.

"Been out?" I asked.

He had been to Wembley Exhibition, he said.

Now Wembley ran a guessing competition. When you entered you received a card on which you wrote down your guess of the number of people who would pay for admission the next day. It was a green card, and was almost the first thing I saw lying on the table.

"There's a chance for a hundred pounds, Sooper," he said, and smiled as he took up the ticket and handed it to me.

"What time were you there?" I asked.

"About four," he said.,

"You're a bit of a motor-cyclist, aren't you?"

He shook his head.

"I've never ridden one," he answered. "Why do you ask?"

Before I could say a word there was a knock on the hall door, and immediately afterwards another knock. I was nearest I went into the hall and opened the door. A woman was standing there, so drenched, so miserably dressed, that I did not recognise her. There was a light on the landing, and she must have recognised me, for she cowered back as if I was going to strike her.

"Come in, Mrs Banford," I said, and slowly she shrank past me into the dining-room where Horace Angel was standing by the table. He said nothing; his wide-opened eyes were staring at her as though she were a ghost

"Hullo…Dora!" he whispered. "My God…how awful!"

She looked as if she had found her dress on a junk heap. It was old and ill-fitting… I remember that there had been a sort of pattern worked in little beads. Some of the pattern was missing. Two or three threads were hanging loose, losing beads with every movement she made. Her hat was like a man's, shapeless and big and dripping from the brim.

"Hullo…Horry!"

The words seemed to strangle her, and though she spoke to him her eyes were on me – big, round, blue eyes, set far back in dark hollows.

"Where have you come from, Mrs Banford?" I asked.

She wore old boots that were soggy with rain and grey with mud; her skirt looked as if it had been soaked in water.

"From Dover… I walked," she said breathlessly. "I've been waiting outside to see you, Horry – I knew you were in London. I went to the Bloomsbury Garage and saw your old motor-bicycle: they said that you had been in two hours."

I looked at Horace Angel – who couldn't ride a motor-bicycle – but he had no eyes for me. He was tugging his handkerchief from his pocket to wipe his streaming face…the handkerchief came out and something else – a white cotton glove that fell on the table. It was the left glove, an exact fellow to the other that had been found in the covert.

I said nothing, waiting… Dora went on:

"I've been in England four days… Jonnes had me put in prison…a French prison."

"Why?"

She shook her head.

"I was mad… I don't know…the knife was on the table and I was mad."

"You attacked him and you were put into a French prison: when?"

She put her hand before her eyes as if she was trying to think.

"A year ago. There was no trial, and when he did not appear to sign some papers they released me. They do that sort of thing in France. They paid my fare, third-class to Dover, and I walked."

"I'm sorry."

Horace Angel was so hoarse that he barked the words. And then she looked at him, I think for the first time.

"Are you? I'm past that, Horry… My God! if that man hadn't come into the wood –!"

"What's that?" I asked sharply. "Which wood?"

She turned her head.

"There's somebody at the door…police…but you're a policeman, aren't you?"

Her numbed fingers snapped back the catch of the shabby bag she carried.

"I don't want this – "

She laid a tiny automatic on the table.

And then the door opened slowly and a woman came in. I must have forgotten to fasten the outer door. It was Mrs Jonnes – she wore an oilskin cloak. I noticed this because she kept her hands hidden under it. Her face was white and her eyes were like red lamps.

"You're Dora Banford," she said.

Dora nodded.

And then the hands came into view and the shot gun. I snatched it from her before her fingers could curl round the trigger, and she dropped into a chair and burst into tears.

I don't exactly remember how I got them all three to the station, but when I got them there it looked as if my trouble was beginning, for who to charge I did not know.

Jonnes' doctor saved me a lot of trouble next morning.

"The man died of heart failure, as I warned him he would," he telephoned me. "The wound was accidental – he probably pulled the trigger as he fell, and anyway it would not have killed a rat."

And so nobody hanged. Not Horace Angel, who went to burgle the safe with a key that he'd pinched or copied years before; not Mrs Jonnes, who came after Dora with murder in her heart; nor Dora, who tramped to Hertford to settle accounts with the man who had broken her.

But the clues – gosh! I'll never get clues like those again!

ROMANCE IN IT

Spending money (said the Superintendent) is an art. Have you ever noticed that when people come into money suddenly the first thing they do is to create criminals? It's a fact. They begin right, but they weaken on it. The feller who buys the winning ticket in the Calcutta Sweep always starts by saying that he's just going to jog along at his old job in the grocery department, and the girl who inherits a million dollars from her uncle in Australia tells the reporter that she wants nothing more than a little cottage in the country with roses up the garden path, but one of 'em ends by playing a system at Monte Carlo and the other finishes up as Queen of the night clubs.

Neither could understand why swells who hadn't a quarter of their money lived twice as well.

You've got to be educated from birth in money-spending: it must be kicked into you at school and at home – it's one of the hardest things a feller can learn.

I knew a bird who never quite learnt it. On the other hand, I know one who did. How many millions he had I've never discovered. Probably none. The moment a man lives in a big house and acts mean, people think he's a millionaire; but certainly Mr Johnson Goott was rich.

He had one child, a girl, and from information received I understand he intended marrying her to a peer of the realm. Instead of which she married a gentleman. I'm not trying to be funny – I know both the fellers. Lord What's-his-name's been married twice since then, and his second divorce is coming up to the courts in the New Year.

Elsie Goott met a young officer at a dance – his name was Fairlight, and so was hers a month after that.

Old Goott said some very unpleasant things about her and her mother, and what happened before she was born when her mother was staying in Scotland, and I hope for the girl's sake he was right, because it was no catch to have a lot of mean Goott blood running through your heart and important blood vessels.

Anyway, he cut her off with nothing and sent her young husband all the bills she'd run up before her marriage.

Captain Fairlight left the army and became a hopeless gambler: in other words, he started a poultry farm. Lot of army gentlemen do this: they like ordering chickens about.

That is how I came to know them. They were on my manor (to use a thieves' expression) when I was in charge of one of the outlying districts of London.

The only man I ever met who understood chickens was a fellow called Linsy, who was the cleverest confidence man in the business. Naturally he would. No chicken could even pretend she could lay eggs with Linsy unless she really could deliver the goods. And when, after knowing the Fairlights for about six months and seeing their stock going down three points a day, I felt it was time to give them a helping hand, I thought of Linsy and went and looked him up.

He was living in a handsome flat in Bayswater, and had a manservant and a maidservant, and maybe an ox and an ass in his back yard. And naturally he was going straight.

"The other game isn't worth the candle, Sooper," he said. "There aren't enough clever people in the world. They have to be clever to be caught – no real fool ever bought a gold brick or trusted you with a wad of notes to show you his confidence in you."

I'm something of a kid myself and fairy stories go a long way with me, but I never believe that any habitual criminal is going straight to anywhere but the Assizes. But I'm a polite man, naturally, and I can look as if I believed anything.

He was interested about the chickens.

"Funny how these amateurs always walk into that graft," he said. "I remember years ago — "

"Don't let's have any reminiscences, Mike," I said. "Can you do anything for these young people? I don't mind introducing you, because there's nothing to be made out of them."

I'd seen his eyes light up at the mention of chickens. It was the one subject he really got enthusiastic about — he was the fellow that started the chicken farm at Parkhurst, or was it Dartmoor?

"Sure, I'll help you," he said. "And you can trust me to give 'em a square deal, unless they've got a breed I specially want, and then I'll try and buy it."

I heard from Mrs Fairlight a few days after, that he'd been down, but it was a month before I saw Linsy.

"That captain fellow knows more than most hen-feeders," he said, "but he hasn't enough capital. He wants a place about ten times as big, and I've told him to buy the farm next door — it's for sale. And he ought to put up some new runs and buy a few of Lord Dewin's prize birds. And he should run a motor-van to carry his stock to market. There's a fortune in that farm, with a fellow like Fairlight. What a woman she is, Sooper! You wouldn't think a so-and-so like Goott would have a daughter…"

I let him rave on, for I knew there was no harm in Linsy. He was naturally romantic; otherwise he wouldn't have been a confidence man, or at any rate a successful confidence man.

She wrote to the old man and asked him to lend her some money. He wrote back telling her he wouldn't, and didn't even put a stamp on the letter.

"Goott," said Linsy thoughtfully, and I could see a look in his eye that wasn't quite lawful.

"Unless you want to find yourself sewing mailbags in Wormwood Scrubbs, keep away from Goott," I warned him. "He's so wide that you can't get past him."

"Those are the kind I like," said Linsy.

Now the funny thing about rich men is that things are always turning up to make them richer. A poor man can dig in his garden all day and never turn up a threepenny bit; but every time a rich man opens his door there's the postman waiting with a registered letter.

Goott had all sorts of successes. He was the only man that ever put money into a treasure-hunting expedition and got a profit on it. If he bought a property in the middle of the Sahara Desert, he'd find gold on it, and a brand-new spring would come up to wash it.

I don't know how he got his start, but I'll bet it was dishonest. He was so wide that even his cook never got a rake-off from the tradesmen. So that when a friend of Linsy's called at Goott's house in Brook Street – Linsy only did the very big jobs himself – with one of Linsy's cleverest little stories about an uncle dying in California and wanting him to distribute the money, Mr Goott didn't wait for the story to finish, but sent for the police. Linsy's friend didn't even wait for the police.

I heard this from Superintendent Bryne, who was in control of that area. From certain peculiarities of the story I knew that Linsy was behind it, because the yarn wasn't as crude as I have made it. I was a little surprised, because Linsy isn't quite a sap, and must have known that that old con yarn could never get over in Brook Street – not at No. 274, anyway.

As a matter of fact, I heard the yarn at first-hand, because I happened to be up west, and I called on Mr Goott. He was a short man with a bald head and a black moustache, and what he didn't say about confidence men he said about the police.

"These fellows don't understand that I can smell money." He spoke with a slightly Dutch accent. "It's an instinct with me."

He seemed unusually excited – I didn't know why. I couldn't guess that the sailor was waiting in the study for him to come back and continue the conversation.

The sailor had arrived that afternoon with a letter in introduction from a man in Leningrad. It was written on a thin piece of tissue paper and hidden in a cigarette, and it was in Dutch.

DEAR FRIEND GOOTT, I want you to see this man. He will tell
you everything.

It was signed "Jan van Roos."

The sailor had a difficulty in meeting Mr Goott, who kept three
people in his house to prevent anybody seeing him. There was the
footman at the door, there was the butler, and there was Mr Goott's
secretary. But the sailor, who didn't look like a sailor because he was
dressed in an old suit of clothes and a Derby hat, got to him at last by
sending in the cigarette and asking him to open it.

The sailor's name was Brown. He had been a member of the crew
of a ship which had gone to Leningrad, and he had been persuaded
by Soviet agents to join their organisation. One night he had been
arrested, and in prison he met van Roos, who used to be a prosperous
diamond merchant but had been for two years in the prison of St
Peter and St Paul. The sailor and van Roos had long conversations. He
had nursed the Dutchman through a sickness, and when, for no reason
at all, they were both released, they were the best of friends.

"What's all this to do with me?" asked Goott, very impatiently.

The man glanced at him angrily. (This is Goott's own description.)

"I don't know how much it's got to do with you," he said gruffly.
"If you don't want to hear it, I won't waste my time any more. But
I've seen the boxes with my own eyes."

Goott had an appointment in the city which he couldn't give up.
He asked the man to call again that night, and he was there in the
study when Bryne and I made our visit – though of course we didn't
know this.

Goott hurried back to the sailor the moment we had gone.

"Listen, my friend," he said. (I am relying entirely on his account
of the conversation: it is probably more or less accurate.) "You tell me
that after, the Revolution the reserves of the Imperial Bank were
packed into six boxes containing English and American banknotes,
and that they were taken to the shores of the Baltic and buried there.
I'm not a fool. Only this night I've seen two police officers who came
to speak to me about another attempting swindler."

Brown got up and took his hat.

"Then I won't say any more to you," he said. "I've told you before what van Roos told me. I've told you I've seen the boxes buried under the floor of an old house, and if you like to come to the place I'm lodging I can show you the plan. I'm not asking for anything, I'm not offering you anything. There's only three people who know about this and one of 'em's dead — that's van Roos. He died the week before I smuggled myself on to a Soviet vessel that was coming to Hull."

"Who's the other man?"

"The Grand Duke Boris," said the sailor. "He's in London, and he's been trying to find me. But van Roos said he was only entitled to a very small share. He wouldn't have any of it if I had my way."

Goott was impressed and agreed to go with the man to his lodgings. He was staying at a small hotel off the Blackfriars Road. But Goott was a careful man.

"I'll go in daylight," he said, and the man offered no objection.

The next afternoon he arrived at the little temperance hotel and was shown up to the sailor's room. It was a poorish kind of apartment: it had nothing in it beyond the furniture except one sea trunk.

He found Brown sitting on the bed in his shirt-sleeves, smoking a pipe. Groott was taking no risks: he had two private detectives outside watching the house, with instructions to come in after him if he wasn't out in a quarter of an hour. To be on the safe side he told Brown this.

"Don't you worry: nobody's going to hurt you. Besides, I'm not wanting your help any more," said the sailor, getting up and stretching himself. "I like dealing with gentlemen who are gentlemen, and when a man doubts my word it makes me mad. I'm very sorry to have troubled you, Mr Goott."

Goott was standing by the window with an eye on the street. He was also visible to the two detectives who had followed him; and at that moment he saw a big Rolls draw up before the hotel, a footman got down and opened the door, and a very elegant-looking swell got out and looked up at the house with an expression on his face as if he smelt something that he didn't like.

"You promised to show me the plan."

"It's not necessary," said Brown. "I'm not doing any more business with you. And besides, I see it's useless trying to get you to help. I'll tell you plainly that it would cost you ten thousand pounds to charter a boat, and anybody with half an eye could see that you wouldn't put up ten thousand pence."

"You're right there," said Goott.

"Well," said the sailor, knocking out the ashes of his pipe in the fire-grate, "we won't talk any more about it. I've offered you a lot of money – I don't know how much it is. Van Roos said it was two millions, but he was probably lying – "

There was a knock at the door, and the sailor looked round, rather startled. He glanced at Goott suspiciously.

"Who's that?" he asked. "One of your pals?"

"No friend of mine," said Goott, getting nearer to the window so that the detectives could see what was happening to him – if anything did happen.

The knock came again.

"Come in," said Brown.

The door opened and there entered the swell whom Goott had seen getting out of the car. He saw the Dutchman and frowned.

"Who is this?" he asked sharply.

The sailor grinned.

"It doesn't matter who it is, your Highness," he said roughly. "A friend of mine if you like."

He looked at Goott and jerked his head towards the swell.

"This is the Grand Duke I've been talking to you about."

"Does this man know?" asked the Grand Duke, breathing hard.

"He knows as much as you know," said Brown. "He knows that there is stuff, but he doesn't know where it is, and nobody else knows until I get a signed agreement with you that I have my share. You tried to beat me down – "

"Then he does know?" interrupted the Grand Duke between his teeth.

Turning, he locked the door and faced the sailor. He was a head taller than Brown and a strong-looking fellow.

"I'll repeat my offer," he said. "I will pay the cost of the expedition, I will guarantee you a hundred thousand pounds – "

"Nothing doing," said the sailor loudly. "I don't know how much stuff is there, but I want half."

The eyes of the Grand Duke half closed, and Goott said he never so much as saw his arm move; but suddenly there appeared in his hand a Browning, with which he covered the sailor.

"More than a half of that money," he said quietly, "is the property of my family. You have the plan – you brought this man to see it. I want it."

Before Goott knew what had happened, the sailor leaped at him like a cat. The pistol dropped from the Grand Duke's hand and he was flung backward across the bed. Goott looked helplessly through the window and saw his detectives, but for a second did not know what to do. But he was a quick thinker. Reaching forward, he jerked the sailor backward. The Grand Duke came to his feet, breathless and pale.

"Let's talk this thing over," said Goott. "We are business men…"

It was a long time before the Grand Duke could speak. Brown was all for making a rough house, but in the end they made an appointment to meet in Brook Street, and about midnight the sailor and the Grand Duke left, the best of friends, with a bearer cheque for ten thousand pounds and one of the three signed agreements that the money should be split three ways.

I ran across Linsy a year after this: he was in the lounge of the Grand Hotel in Paris. I had gone over to bring back a fellow who had swindled the Midland Bank. It was only just before I left that I heard all this from Mr Goott, because naturally he was sore and didn't want everybody to know that he had backed a loser.

"If you say it was me, it was me," said Linsy, "but you've got to prove it. If you say that the Grand Duke was young Allison – why, you'd better ask him. If you tell me you've been down to the Fairlights and that I lent them the money to buy the farm, that doesn't prove anything either. I can only tell you this, Sooper, that the cleverer a man is the easier he is to catch, if you can put a little bit of romance into the catching."

A few months later I was introduced to an American gentleman who wanted to know all about Linsy. He pointed to Linsy as he crossed the hall.

"You see that man?" he said. "I will tell you in confidence that he's working for the King of Siam, and he's found a big emerald mine…"

Edgar Wallace

Big Foot

Footprints and a dead woman bring together Superintendent Minton and the amateur sleuth Mr Cardew. Who is the man in the shrubbery? Who is the singer of the haunting Moorish tune? Why is Hannah Shaw so determined to go to Pawsy, 'a dog lonely place' she had previously detested? Death lurks in the dark and someone must solve the mystery before BIG FOOT strikes again, in a yet more fiendish manner.

Bones In London

The new Managing Director of Schemes Ltd has an elegant London office and a theatrically dressed assistant – however, Bones, as he is better known, is bored. Luckily there is a slump in the shipping market and it is not long before Joe and Fred Pole pay Bones a visit. They are totally unprepared for Bones' unnerving style of doing business, unprepared for his unique style of innocent and endearing mischief.

Edgar Wallace

Bones of the River

'Taking the little paper from the pigeon's leg, Hamilton saw it was from Sanders and marked URGENT. *Send Bones instantly to Lujamalababa... Arrest and bring to headquarters the witch doctor.*'

It is a time when the world's most powerful nations are vying for colonial honour, a time of trading steamers and tribal chiefs. In the mysterious African territories administered by Commissioner Sanders, Bones persistently manages to create his own unique style of innocent and endearing mischief.

The Daffodil Mystery

When Mr Thomas Lyne, poet, poseur and owner of Lyne's Emporium insults a cashier, Odette Rider, she resigns. Having summoned detective Jack Tarling to investigate another employee, Mr Milburgh, Lyne now changes his plans. Tarling and his Chinese companion refuse to become involved. They pay a visit to Odette's flat and in the hall Tarling meets Sam, convicted felon and protégé of Lyne. Next morning Tarling discovers a body. The hands are crossed on the breast, adorned with a handful of daffodils.

EDGAR WALLACE

THE JOKER
(USA: THE COLOSSUS)

While the millionaire Stratford Harlow is in Princetown, not only does he meet with his lawyer Mr Ellenbury but he gets his first glimpse of the beautiful Aileen Rivers, niece of the actor and convicted felon Arthur Ingle. When Aileen is involved in a car accident on the Thames Embankment, the driver is James Carlton of Scotland Yard. Later that evening Carlton gets a call. It is Aileen. She needs help.

THE SQUARE EMERALD
(USA: THE GIRL FROM SCOTLAND YARD)

'Suicide on the left,' says Chief Inspector Coldwell pleasantly, as he and Leslie Maughan stride along the Thames Embankment during a brutally cold night. A gaunt figure is sprawled across the parapet. But Coldwell soon discovers that Peter Dawlish, fresh out of prison for forgery, is not considering suicide but murder. Coldwell suspects Druze as the intended victim. Maughan disagrees. If Druze dies, she says, 'It will be because he does not love children!'

OTHER TITLES BY EDGAR WALLACE AVAILABLE DIRECT
FROM HOUSE OF STRATUS

Quantity		£	$(US)	$(CAN)	€
	THE ADMIRABLE CARFEW	6.99	12.95	19.95	13.50
	THE ANGEL OF TERROR	6.99	12.95	19.95	13.50
	THE AVENGER *(USA: THE HAIRY ARM)*	6.99	12.95	19.95	13.50
	BARBARA ON HER OWN	6.99	12.95	19.95	13.50
	BIG FOOT	6.99	12.95	19.95	13.50
	THE BLACK ABBOT	6.99	12.95	19.95	13.50
	BONES	6.99	12.95	19.95	13.50
	BONES IN LONDON	6.99	12.95	19.95	13.50
	BONES OF THE RIVER	6.99	12.95	19.95	13.50
	THE CLUE OF THE NEW PIN	6.99	12.95	19.95	13.50
	THE CLUE OF THE SILVER KEY	6.99	12.95	19.95	13.50
	THE CLUE OF THE TWISTED CANDLE	6.99	12.95	19.95	13.50
	THE COAT OF ARMS				
	(USA: THE ARRANWAYS MYSTERY)	6.99	12.95	19.95	13.50
	THE COUNCIL OF JUSTICE	6.99	12.95	19.95	13.50
	THE CRIMSON CIRCLE	6.99	12.95	19.95	13.50
	THE DAFFODIL MYSTERY	6.99	12.95	19.95	13.50
	THE DARK EYES OF LONDON				
	(USA: THE CROAKERS)	6.99	12.95	19.95	13.50
	THE DAUGHTERS OF THE NIGHT	6.99	12.95	19.95	13.50
	A DEBT DISCHARGED	6.99	12.95	19.95	13.50
	THE DEVIL MAN	6.99	12.95	19.95	13.50
	THE DOOR WITH SEVEN LOCKS	6.99	12.95	19.95	13.50
	THE DUKE IN THE SUBURBS	6.99	12.95	19.95	13.50
	THE FACE IN THE NIGHT	6.99	12.95	19.95	13.50
	THE FEATHERED SERPENT	6.99	12.95	19.95	13.50
	THE FLYING SQUAD	6.99	12.95	19.95	13.50
	THE FORGER *(USA: THE CLEVER ONE)*	6.99	12.95	19.95	13.50
	THE FOUR JUST MEN	6.99	12.95	19.95	13.50
	FOUR SQUARE JANE	6.99	12.95	19.95	13.50

ALL HOUSE OF STRATUS BOOKS ARE AVAILABLE FROM GOOD BOOKSHOPS
OR DIRECT FROM THE PUBLISHER:

Internet: **www.houseofstratus.com** including synopses and features.
Email: **sales@houseofstratus.com**
              info@houseofstratus.com
              (please quote author, title and credit card details.)

OTHER TITLES BY EDGAR WALLACE AVAILABLE DIRECT
FROM HOUSE OF STRATUS

Quantity		£	$(US)	$(CAN)	€
☐	THE FOURTH PLAGUE	6.99	12.95	19.95	13.50
☐	THE FRIGHTENED LADY	6.99	12.95	19.95	13.50
☐	GOOD EVANS	6.99	12.95	19.95	13.50
☐	THE HAND OF POWER	6.99	12.95	19.95	13.50
☐	THE IRON GRIP	6.99	12.95	19.95	13.50
☐	THE JOKER (USA: THE COLOSSUS)	6.99	12.95	19.95	13.50
☐	THE JUST MEN OF CORDOVA	6.99	12.95	19.95	13.50
☐	THE KEEPERS OF THE KING'S PEACE	6.99	12.95	19.95	13.50
☐	THE LAW OF THE FOUR JUST MEN	6.99	12.95	19.95	13.50
☐	THE MAN WHO BOUGHT LONDON	6.99	12.95	19.95	13.50
☐	THE MAN WHO KNEW	6.99	12.95	19.95	13.50
☐	THE MAN WHO WAS NOBODY	6.99	12.95	19.95	13.50
☐	THE MIND OF MR J G REEDER				
	(USA: THE MURDER BOOK OF J G REEDER)	6.99	12.95	19.95	13.50
☐	MORE EDUCATED EVANS	6.99	12.95	19.95	13.50
☐	MR J G REEDER RETURNS				
	(USA: MR REEDER RETURNS)	6.99	12.95	19.95	13.50
☐	MR JUSTICE MAXELL	6.99	12.95	19.95	13.50
☐	RED ACES	6.99	12.95	19.95	13.50
☐	ROOM 13	6.99	12.95	19.95	13.50
☐	SANDERS	6.99	12.95	19.95	13.50
☐	SANDERS OF THE RIVER	6.99	12.95	19.95	13.50
☐	THE SINISTER MAN	6.99	12.95	19.95	13.50
☐	THE SQUARE EMERALD				
	(USA: THE GIRL FROM SCOTLAND YARD)	6.99	12.95	19.95	13.50
☐	THE THREE JUST MEN	6.99	12.95	19.95	13.50
☐	THE THREE OAK MYSTERY	6.99	12.95	19.95	13.50
☐	THE TRAITOR'S GATE	6.99	12.95	19.95	13.50
☐	WHEN THE GANGS CAME TO LONDON	6.99	12.95	19.95	13.50

Tel:	**Order Line** **0800 169 1780** (UK) **800 724 1100** (USA) **International** **+44 (0) 1845 527700** (UK) **+01 845 463 1100** (USA)
Fax:	**+44 (0) 1845 527711** (UK) **+01 845 463 0018** (USA) (please quote author, title and credit card details.)
Send to:	**House of Stratus Sales Department** **Thirsk Industrial Park** **York Road, Thirsk** **North Yorkshire, YO7 3BX** **UK**

PAYMENT

Please tick currency you wish to use:

☐ £ (Sterling)   ☐ $ (US)   ☐ $ (CAN)   ☐ € (Euros)

Allow for shipping costs charged per order plus an amount per book as set out in the tables below:

CURRENCY/DESTINATION

	£(Sterling)	$(US)	$(CAN)	€ (Euros)
Cost per order				
UK	1.50	2.25	3.50	2.50
Europe	3.00	4.50	6.75	5.00
North America	3.00	3.50	5.25	5.00
Rest of World	3.00	4.50	6.75	5.00
Additional cost per book				
UK	0.50	0.75	1.15	0.85
Europe	1.00	1.50	2.25	1.70
North America	1.00	1.00	1.50	1.70
Rest of World	1.50	2.25	3.50	3.00

PLEASE SEND CHEQUE OR INTERNATIONAL MONEY ORDER
payable to: HOUSE OF STRATUS LTD or HOUSE OF STRATUS INC. or card payment as indicated

STERLING EXAMPLE

Cost of book(s):..................... Example: 3 x books at £6.99 each: £20.97

Cost of order: .... Example: £1.50 (Delivery to UK address)

Additional cost per book:.............. Example: 3 x £0.50: £1.50

Order total including shipping:.......... Example: £23.97

VISA, MASTERCARD, SWITCH, AMEX:

☐☐☐☐☐☐☐☐☐☐☐☐☐☐☐☐☐☐☐☐

Issue number (Switch only):

☐☐☐

Start Date: **Expiry Date:**

☐☐/ ☐☐   ☐☐/ ☐☐

Signature: _____

NAME: _____

ADDRESS: _____

COUNTRY: _____

ZIP/POSTCODE: _____

Please allow 28 days for delivery. Despatch normally within 48 hours.

Prices subject to change without notice.
Please tick box if you do not wish to receive any additional information. ☐

House of Stratus publishes many other titles in this genre; please check our website (**www.houseofstratus.com**) for more details.